# Her Unexpected Cowboy

## Unforgettable Cowboys Book One

DANAE LITTLE

# DEDICATION

To all who dare to wish for the unexpected

# ACKNOWLEDGMENTS

I want to thank everyone who has been a part of my writing journey, from my editor, beta readers, ARC readers, and family to the people who I meet who might unknowingly spark a new story in my mind.

Join Danae's **Reader Group** for new releases and a FREE book!

Yellow light flickered in the small room, causing shadows to grow and shrink. Beads of wax rolled lazily down the candles and melted into the chocolate frosting on the homemade cake. Sydney sighed, causing the flame to wiggle in a frantic dance.

"Well, happy birthday to me," she said in resignation. "Twenty-eight years old…"

"Meow." A black and white cat sat in the chair next to her, blinking his yellow eyes in the dim light before stretching and jumping onto her lap.

"What's that, Mr. Paws?" She stroked her companion. "I need to make a wish?"

"Meow," Mr. Paws confirmed.

A chuckle bubbled up through Sydney. If her old friends could only see her now. In her defense, Mr. Paws could actually hold a decent conversation. Her laughter died as she rested her chin in her calloused hands. The wax melted, drip, drip, drip, polka-dotting the cake with small pink and blue spots.

This was the second birthday that she had spent alone on the ranch. Her heart squeezed in the grip of loneliness now so much more than the first. That first year here had been an answered prayer, a perfect escape from the nightmare her life had become. Sydney silently sent thanks to her Aunty Mag and Uncle Joe for leaving her this place.

Sydney had always enjoyed her summers here as a kid. Working with the goats and horses, and having the freedom to run and be alone gave her the strength to make it through the rest of the year. She never thought she would get to the point that being alone would feel, well, so lonely.

"Meow." Mr. Paws arched up and put his white socked paws on her chest to touch noses.

"I'm so grateful to have you." Sydney touched his wet nose with hers, relishing in his methodic rumbling of a purr.

A deep bellow of a bark traveled from the porch. A shaggy bear of a dog stood at the screen door and let out a grumble as he circled twice before finally dropping into a pile of white fur.

"Yes, I'm grateful for you too, Guardian." Sydney loved having the door open to let the fresh spring night air into the small stuffy house. Plus, it let her interact more with Guardian. She rubbed her hand down the cat's sleek fur. "Silly dog," she whispered. "Always acts like he's left out."

"Meow."

"I know…a wish."

Another sigh escaped. The purring from her lap, the crickets outside, and the occasional bleat from the goats,— all music to Sydney's ears, settled her. A wistful smile spread across her lips. "Well, since it's only you and me."

"Woof," Guardian added.

"And Guardian, too, of course. I can be as silly and fanciful as I desire." Sydney's heart ached as a sad wash of desperation flooded her. "Okay, I wish that a tall, dark, handsome man…"

"Meow."

"Yes, I know that's a cliché. Okay, with magnificent green eyes and large hands." She looked towards Mr. Paws for approval, and he nodded as he began licking his paw. "In a cowboy hat," she huffed at her absurdity, "would show up here, sweep me off my feet, want to live in this old cozy house, love goats and horses, and of course you and Guardian, enjoy hard work, and this simple life." She hesitated and checked her mental list of attributes of her perfect man.

"Meow."

"Oh, yes, of course we fall madly in love with each other." With a deep breath, feeling quite senseless and despondent, she blew out the candles which, by now, only stood a half-inch off the cake. If her wish didn't show up at her door, she would have to leave this ranch and the tiny town it lived in to find Mr. Right. The only options here were grizzled old men who looked like remnants of the fur-trapper days, a toothless drunk, a few punk kids, and, well, she couldn't forget, a married man.

"Meow."

"Oh, you're right, Mr. Paws. I forgot to add in that he would be respectful, kind, honest, and not an all-round loser."

"Woof-woof."

"Thank you for the reminder, Guardian, and not in trouble with the law." Her face scrunched up in memories she didn't want to stay in. "Too bad I already blew out the candles."

"Woof-woof."

"I know, Guardian. I know." Sydney slowly took the candles out and sucked the chocolate frosting off the bottoms.

Guardian continued barking, more adamantly. Pricks of anxiety encouraged Sydney to investigate what caused his trouble as a deep growl emanated from him. Guardian didn't growl unless.... She would have heard a car come down the long, gravel driveway. The goats were quiet except for the occasional bleat. Whinny neighed and stamped her feet, but the crickets—they were silent.

Her hair stood up on end and her heart hammered. Maybe the wolves had returned or that dang bear that liked to spread trash from here to the barn. Her hand grasped the cold metal barrel of her uncle's old shotgun just as she heard what sounded like a boot grating on gravel.

In an instant, she brought the butt of the gun into the familiar calloused nook of her shoulder. At that moment the automatic sensor lights blazed to life, illuminating a man standing just off the porch who quickly shielded his eyes. The breath caught in Sydney's throat. Thank God, she wasn't a screamer, because this was definitely a screamable moment!

"Stop," Sydney choked out, trying to get a lung-full of air. With a deep breath, she firmly planted her feet on the hardwood floor. "Stop right there." Adrenaline stung her skin. She prayed she would have the courage to do what needed to be done.

The man froze, still shielding his eyes. He held his body in a peculiar way, closed in on itself, arm held tight to his chest and one leg awkwardly straight, slightly kicked out to the side. The outside light passed shadows over him, hiding his features, though the dark couldn't hide his size, neither could his posture. Broad shoulders filled in his black t-shirt. He must have stood around six foot at least. A fraction of a chiseled jaw peeked out from out of the shadow and into the light as he shifted his weight.

"I'm sorry, Ma'am." His voice crackled as if he hadn't used it in some time. He cleared his throat, causing him to take in a sharp breath. "I didn't mean to frighten you." He spoke through gritted teeth.

"Where did you come from? Where's your car?" she shot the questions at him.

He wavered before steadying himself. "I don't know."

"You're hurt," she stated.

"Yeah." A slight pain-filled chuckle traveled across the cool evening breeze.

"I'll call the Sheriff and maybe an ambulance," she said, backing up towards the table where the phone sat next to her cake. She had thought for sure at least her parents would have called today. She shook her head, refocusing on the issue at hand.

"No," he said quickly. He took a couple steps forward, placing a foot on the lowest step of the porch.

Guardian picked up his incessant growling with more

fervor. Sydney's heart raced as she squared the gun towards the man's chest again.

"Please," he pleaded, his one good hand moving away from shielding his eyes and outstretched towards her.

Blood rushed through her as she saw his face for the first time. *Handsome…so handsome.* The gun slowly lowered as she stared, mesmerized by his eyes still dark in the shadow.

"I don't want to be trouble," his words soothed, sounding as if he were taming a wild horse. He turned slightly towards the barn a hundred yards or so past the house. "I…If you don't mind, I could just sleep the night in your barn."

Sydney glanced at the outbuilding, knowing full well that she had two mother goats in there about to give birth and no bed. She thought about Homer, the grizzled old foreman, a half-mile down the road. She could send this stranger there. Watching him, though, she wasn't sure he could make it

"Just tonight," he soothed again.

"You should see a doctor, at the least," she said, hesitantly. *Why in the world aren't you calling the sheriff right now?!* Her good sense continued to yell at her while she studied his strong jawline and high cheekbones. His dark, short hair stood out all over the place, somehow making him even more attractive.

"I'll be fine, just banged up." He wavered again, and this time he reached out to the railing to steady himself.

As if pulled by an unseen force, Sydney reached for the screen door and stepped out, the gun still nestled in her shoulder, but pointed towards the ground. Guardian backed up to shield her, his low growl menacing.

"Quite the dog you have there," the man said, his voice fading and his knuckles turning white as he squeezed the splintered railing.

Sydney couldn't stop staring at the size of his hand. Thick, long fingers and a palm that would put that pesky bear to shame. She snuck a glance at Guardian—his white, furry head came to her waist, and his fist-sized paws stood in a wide ready-to-pounce stance. He was an intimidating view.

"Yes, and very loyal," she replied accentuating the very part—which he was. With Guardian around, she didn't fear for almost anything. Yet this man wavering in front of her scared the pants off her, in more ways than one. Her heart thundered and she fought to breath every time their eyes connected. What was it about this cowboy that made her fear more for her heart than her life?

The man nodded. With his eyes never leaving hers, he slowly lowered himself to the step at the bottom of the porch. A burst of air left him, as if he desired to blow his pain out onto the wind. Then he scanned the land intensely.

Sydney followed his eyes, seeing the silver of moonlight touch the top of the lodgepole pines beyond the clearing and glinting off the metal roof of the barn. The crickets had picked up their song once again. A peace filled her, even in the midst of this scary, crazy situation. This was her land…her home.

"Are you going to tell me what happened?" she asked, fully on the porch now, only a good twenty feet from the alluring stranger.

His eyes dropped from the landscape to his jeans which were covered in dirt. "I, uh, I can't remember."

"Hmmf," she said. Now that's a lame line. "Fine. We'll play it your way, and Sheriff Whitmore will be out here to help jog that memory of yours."

"Whitmore?" he questioned in a pondering whisper.

"Yeah," she said with a bit of attitude. The sheriff, Wil Whitmore, had once been a hired hand on this ranch as a teenager. They had spent time working together during the summers she spent here. Goosebumps crept on her skin thinking of him. Had Wil really changed that much or had she just been a naïve young girl?

"What county are we in?" The stranger in front of her asked, bringing her back to the situation at hand.

"Mountain Valley."

"Huh." He shook his head slightly before quickly bringing his hand to his head. When he moved it away, his fingers glistened in the porch light.

"That's a nasty cut you got there."

He looked down at the blood on his hand. "Yeah, guess that's not good."

Without thought she turned back into the house and filled up a baggie with ice. *What are you doing, Sydney? There's a beat up stranger on your porch, and you are getting him a bag of ice instead of calling Wil?* Her hands froze in mid zip of the bag…there was just something about the stranger.

"Meow." Mr. Paws rubbed between her feet before stretching up to get more pets. Absentmindedly, she squatted down to pet the cat.

*The gun! Where did I leave the gun? You stupid girl!*

She took two long strides back to the screen door. Relief washed over her when she saw the shotgun leaned against the frame, right where she left it. She snuck a peek at the man who had leaned back against the railing, his eyes shut. He really was quite the specimen…and she did make that wish. A frantic giggle escaped her lips before she shot a hand over her mouth.

The sound stirred the man on the porch, and he looked towards her as she made her way out the door.

"Here," she said lamely, handing him the bag of ice. The tips of his fingers grazed hers as he took the bag. Sparks ignited and rushed throughout her in a most pleasant way, in a way she hadn't felt for a long time.

"Thank you." A small grin tugged at the right side of his mouth. He raised his eyes up to hers, and for the first time she was close enough to actually see them.

Her heart froze and her breath caught in her throat. Staring back at her were the greenest eyes she had ever seen. She took a step back, a hand on her heart, and took another and another until her back hit the screen. Guardian, now calm, glanced up at her, letting out a single woof.

*Yeah, yeah, I know,* she silently responded to him.

"What?" the man asked, an endearing furrow scrunching between his eyebrows. "Do you recognize me or something?" His voice came out hesitant, almost awkward.

"No, no." She shook her head, still dazed in disbelief. "Should I?"

"I just hoped you did." He placed the bag of ice on his head. A small grimace lined his face, and he closed his eyes.

"You really don't know what happened," she said, her mouth dropping open. "Do you know what state you are in?"

He gingerly shook his head. "No."

"Do you know if you were driving?"

"No."

"Do you know if you were alone?"

"No."

"Do you know what month it is, or year? Do you know how old you are? Do you even know your own name?"

"No."

"Wow." Her mind reeled with what that must feel like—to have no memory at all.

"Do you always ask this many questions?" The right side of his mouth turned up again.

"Yeah," she admitted while a deep blush burned her cheeks. "What *do* you remember?"

He sat forward and scanned the area again as if he expected someone or something to come crashing through the forest. "I woke up amongst some brush on the side of the road about a half-mile left of your driveway. You really do live out in the boonies."

A smile eased across her face. Yes, she did, and she loved it that way…at least, usually.

He rested back against the railing again. Exhaustion lined his face.

She judged he was probably in his early thirties. His shirt, besides dirty and rumpled, looked like an ordinary shirt. His jeans, ripped and caked in dirt, were Wranglers, which ninety percent of Wyoming wore. His boots, though scuffed and muddy, were fancier than a ranch hand's or pretty much anyone in this small town. He was definitely from this part of the country but those boots placed him as city.

"That's it?" She leaned against the railing opposite of him.

"I walked down your extensive driveway, and here I am." His voice sounded full of defeat, and she found herself yearning for his soothing horseman's tone to return.

"How about a wallet or ID?" she kept trying.

"Checked. Nothing." He opened his eyes again and used his good hand to raise up the shirt sleeve of his left arm. "I have this tattoo. It looks military."

Her mouth hung open. The tattoo on his gun of an arm definitely looked military. It had two swords overlapping each other. Yet, it was the muscle bulging underneath it that had her tongue-tied.

"You checked yourself for tattoos?" The thought burst forth, untying her tongue in a not-so-convenient way.

"Well, not all of me." He eased back again with that one-sided grin.

*Could there be more tattoos hidden on him?* The thought raced through her, speeding up her heartbeat and causing her cheeks to burn again. Thank goodness he had closed his eyes. She watched him, wondering where he came from and why he was out here, and looking like he got the crap beat out of him. Was he in some kind of trouble?

Her heart hammered. Strangely, no gripping fear filled her when she thought of this stranger, at least not of him harming her. Her eyes scanned the land that lay beyond in the darkness and she bristled. Were the men that did this to him still out there somewhere?

"Ma'am?" His voice was weak, dripping exhaustion. "If you have decided to let me stay, I better make my way to the barn before I can't."

"One more question."

That sideways grin made another appearance. How could she be frightened of a man who had such an amiable smile?

"Why don't you want me to call the sheriff?"

"I don't know." He leaned forward and met her with those intensely green eyes. Her insides melted, burning in a deep fire. "It doesn't feel right. I know that sounds crazy, but I just can't place it. I just know I shouldn't involve local law enforcement."

*Local law enforcement? Who talks like that?* She shrugged.

If this guy had something to hide, surely he would have spun some elaborate tale. Her shoulders relaxed as tension eased from her. She didn't really want to deal with Wil tonight anyway. Besides, what harm could this man do sleeping with Pearl and Josie? Though if their time comes, he wouldn't be getting much sleep. Neither of them would.

"I'll get a blanket." She rose and stashed the gun next to the front door before searching the closet for a few blankets. Though the days had become warmer, the nights were still chilly up in the Wyoming foothills. With blankets in hand, she grabbed a bottle of water, some goat cheese, and crackers. "What is wrong with you? He's not a guest!" she admonished.

"What did you say, Ma'am?"

"Do you like goat cheese?" She slammed her face down into the blankets in her arms. *You are so crazy!*

"Uh, I'm not sure but I'm starving enough to try it if you're offering."

Sydney put some cheese, crackers, and a couple of tangerines in a Tupperware container, and as a last thought she sliced a piece of the birthday cake and slipped it in there as well. She might as well share it with someone.

~*~

The rough railings on the deck allowed him just enough support to keep him conscious. His body throbbed, yet something told him this wasn't the first time he had pushed through pain like this.

The woman, who had greeted him with the gun shoved into her shoulder as if it lived there, intrigued him. She muttered to herself again as she moved around in her house. Knowing that she would allow him to sleep in her barn allowed him to breathe easier, if he could. He hoped the pain in his chest was only bruised ribs, and not broken.

When she returned outside, arms laden, he pushed himself to stand, though quite unsteadily with his teeth bared against the pain. He blew out a breath as he looked up. Their eyes met, and he couldn't stop the rush that raced through his veins.

"You know you have…" He stopped himself, cleared his throat, and reached for the items in her hands with his good arm. "Thank you." This wasn't a dating scene. He could be putting her in danger. He didn't need to make her feel uncomfortable by telling her she had the most amazingly multi-colored eyes.

She nodded as he took the blankets from her.

This woman walked with purpose as she led him towards the barn. Though each of her movements enveloped the feminine, she held herself with a confidence he didn't remember most women having. Though, he couldn't remember anything right now. He had no business looking at this Good Samaritan in any way besides as an angel that graced him hospitality.

She hesitated a moment and glanced back at the house. He realized then that she didn't have her shotgun on her. He wished he could say something that would make her realize that she was safe with him, that she had nothing to fear from him. Yet, was that the truth?

Uneasiness made his stomach clench as he scanned the

area. The line of trees, though good protection, could also hide enemies. Enemies…why had he constantly been thinking that since he woke on the side of the road?

He entered the barn behind her. She switched on fluorescent lights that flickered from high in the rafters. Shadows cast along four stalls and a large open area before it closed off rooms at the back. Too many places for people to hide.

Soft bleats grabbed his attention, and he saw two soft muzzles stick through slats of the pens.

"Hello girls, how are you mamas doing? No babies yet?" The woman's voice had softened when addressing the animals. The gentleness created a yearning within him as his heart tugged and squeezed.

"Babies?" he said through gritted teeth. Exhaustion filled him. If he didn't sit down soon, he would fall down.

She turned to look at him and froze as if she had forgotten how to breathe.

He felt the same way, and for a moment his pain and exhaustion fled him. In the light of the barn he saw her eyes that much more clearly—multi-colored like a puzzle perfectly fit together. Her parted lips were smooth and cherry red, and the spattering of freckles across her nose gave her a childlike quality that made him want to protect her.

"Oh, yeah." She cleared her throat and blinked. "These gals are due any day now."

"I see." The moment had been broken and the pain lanced through him even more ferociously. He leaned against the pen as he felt the blood drain from his face.

He must look like he was about to drop, because she took the blankets from him and hastily made her way down to the unoccupied end stall. After laying out a few horse blankets on top of some fresh straw, she set the blankets from the house on top.

When he made it to her, she looked from the makeshift bed to him, back towards the house, and back to him again. She shook her head and muttered to herself again.

"Do you talk to yourself like this all the time?" he asked, feeling his mouth crook up and eyes crinkle.

"Comes with the territory, I guess." She smiled sheepishly before looking to the makeshift bed. "It's no five-star hotel but, your accommodations sir."

"I appreciate this, ma'am."

"Sydney," she said quickly.

"Sydney." He let her name roll around on his tongue before gingerly lowering himself onto the blankets before he passed out on them. She was a great distraction, but his body demanded rest, and demanded it now.

"Here, some food and water." She handed him the Tupperware and a bottle of water.

"Thank you." He looked at the contents and another grin crossed his face. "Cake?"

"Yeah, I, uh, its," she stuttered, "cake." A blush filled her cheeks, and he wished it was brighter so he could see if it would wash out her freckles. She turned from him, disappearing into one of the rooms.

He took the moment to close his eyes and struggled to open them as she tromped back into the stall, his five-star accommodations for the night.

"We should bandage that cut," she said matter-of-factly.

He nodded. All he really wanted was sleep, but how could he tell the kind lady…Sydney, no?

She kneeled down next to him and opened up a metal first aid kit. The spray stung like fire, but he only clenched his teeth against it. Her fingers covered the cut with ointment, gentle and self-assured.

"At least it won't get infected. I don't think it'll need stitches," she said as she finished taping the bandage on and backed up quickly like she couldn't breathe next to him.

He wondered if he stunk, or if she was really that frightened of him. "Thank you."

She nodded and closed up the kit. "Do you need anything else looked at?"

"Not tonight. I appreciate this," he said, though his eyes kept trying to close.

"Well, good night. Hope you, uh, can remember some things in the morning." She backed away until she ran into the gate. "Lights are here, when you're ready."

"Thank you, Sydney. Sleep well, and lock your door." His statement felt inadequate. He lifted a hand in farewell as she fled the barn, practically tripping over her bodyguard of a dog.

As soon as he heard her feet creak up her old porch, he opened the Tupperware and swallowed large chunks of food. How long had it been since he'd eaten? The cheese had a strange aftertaste, but nothing he couldn't get used to. Right now, just having food in his belly made everything taste as delicious as the chocolate cake.

As he picked up the dessert, he noticed a hole and a few specks of pink wax. A birthday cake. The thought tugged on his heart. He looked in the direction of the house as if he could see through the walls. Had that woman spent her birthday alone?

He had noted immediately that she was the sole occupant of the house, and surmised that it wasn't just a temporary thing. He could be wrong. Her spouse could be gone for the night, but he sensed she lived here on the ranch alone. What would ever coerce a woman like her to be so far from society and run a ranch by herself?

The thoughts mulled around in his fuzzy brain as he chowed down the cake. It soon was gone, as was any energy for thoughts. He lay back against the blankets that smelled of memories he couldn't place. A sigh escaped him as he realized the makeshift bed actually was quite comfortable.

His eyes closed immediately. For a moment more he categorized all the sounds he heard: the mother goats shifting around their stalls, more goats bleating occasionally from the pasture, the occasional stomp from horses somewhere beyond the barn, and, most importantly, the crickets.

The world around him seemed at peace, ready to wrap up another day. He would have to trust that his instincts, or the animals, would rouse him if needed. With that thought, sleep overtook him in a hazy, almost drugged-induced way.

# ~2~

There were twenty-six stars outside Sydney's bedroom window. She had been counting them for the last several hours. The almost moonless sky made the perfect night for stargazing. Once again she mentally checked to make sure she had locked the door. Reaching out a hand to touch cold steel reassured her that the shotgun leaned against the nightstand within reach.

"Meow." Mr. Paws sensed her movement.

"Yes, kitty. I know, I should be sleeping." How could she though? The night replayed over and over. She felt in total awe of the coincidence. Yet, what had Aunty Mag always said—*There are no such things as coincidences—only perfect timing.*

Could that handsome, green-eyed devil in the barn really be perfect timing? Sydney covered her face dramatically with a pillow. She just needed to sleep! Was the nameless stranger sleeping right now? Did he snore?

She threw the pillow across the room, spooking Mr. Paws who skittered across the bed and out the door, claws desperately seeking purchase on the slippery wood floor.

Thunk!

Sydney cringed, *Poor Mr. Paws.* Guilt flooded her. She hated when he slid into the walls.

Sitting up with her feet dangling off the queen bed, she stretched and looked out into the night. From the window she couldn't see the barn, but she wondered if the light would still be on. She slipped cold toes into the soft slipper boots and shuffled out to the kitchen.

Maybe some warm milk would help her fall asleep. Aunty Mag always heated some goat milk when she couldn't sleep during her summers here as a child. They would sit on the porch, sipping at their mugs and counting the stars.

A sigh escaped her. She looked longingly at the faded picture that hung on the living room wall and touched Aunty Mag's smiling face. She and Uncle Joe looked so happy on their wedding day. Sydney used to ask her to tell the story of that day over and over while she stared at this picture.

A story of true love—every little girl's dream. Uncle Joe was Aunty Mag's knight in shining armor, but she was no ordinary princess. No, Aunty Mag would never have qualified as princess material, but Uncle Joe sure did do his best to treat her as the queen she was. Their relationship was so different from Sydney's parents.

She turned to pull back the sheer curtain at the front of the house. Her breath caught when she saw the light in the barn still leaking out between the wooden planks. Was the stranger still awake too? She dropped the curtain and took two steps back into the kitchen. The wooden floor squeaked making her heart quicken. When something lightly brushed across her ankles she jumped, and the sharp pierces of adrenaline shot through her.

"Meow."

"Mr. Paws!" she admonished, breathing deeply to quell her racing heart. Bending down, she stroked the cat's fur, letting the repetitive motion soothe her.

Once she had calmed and could breathe freely once again, she opened the fridge, illuminating the kitchen in its glow. The glass pitcher of goat milk felt cool in her hands as she poured some into a mug. Aunty would always warm it up on the stove, but she didn't have the patience for that. The microwave hum seemed loud in the dark, quiet house.

She snuck another peak at the glowing barn while the goat milk heated. The cowboy probably just passed out before he had the chance to turn the lights off. That gash in his head looked horrid. What if he had a concussion? Maybe she should go check on him?

*Ding.*

Saved by the bell. She shook her head as she let go of the curtain again. With the warm mug in hand, she traipsed back to bed, mumbling chastises the whole way.

The milk worked beautifully. So beautifully, in fact, that when Guardian began his morning wake-up call, it left Sydney startled, sitting up abruptly with fuzzy vision. She rubbed her eyes, trying to get them to focus as she stumbled her way to the tiny bathroom. The cool water soothed her sleep-puffy face. She let the droplets drip back into the sink.

Looking up at her reflection, she noticed how dark her lashes looked dripping wet. Her multi-hued eyes stared back at her. She never knew what to say when asked the color of her eyes. They weren't blue, yet not really green, and brown would be pushing it way too far. Rather they had flecks of each of the colors with some gold mixed in to boot.

She had always craved to have green eyes, bright green eyes—like the nameless cowboy in her barn. Her breath caught as memories flooded her. Her wish. The man. The barn. Oh man… The world started to turn black before she finally remembered to breathe again.

Would he still be there? She hastily brushed her teeth, pulled the mess of brown hair up into a pony, and ran back into the bedroom to dress. Guardian barked again.

"I hear ya, buddy. I'm getting your breakfast. Hold your horses," she called out to the impatient dog as Mr. Paws crisscrossed between her legs. "Yes, you too."

She started the coffee pot and continued her routine of feeding the house animals, all while wishing she could run towards the barn to see if her visitor still existed. It hadn't been a dream, had it?

Opening the door, Guardian greeted her with a quiet woof and a huge wagging tail. "Here you go boy, did you sleep good? No other trespassers?" She scratched him behind the ears, sneaking glances towards the barn. The goats and horses loudly requested their breakfasts as well.

When the last blast of coffee steam puffed out, she went back into the house and poured coffee into a commuter mug that she would traipse all around the ranch with until she returned for her own breakfast. She almost made it out the door before going back and pouring another cup of coffee.

It wouldn't hurt to give the man a cup of coffee before she sent him along his way, right?

Her heart raced as she walked across the yard towards the barn. Guardian, already having inhaled his food, followed at her heels. Would the man still be there? Where did he come from? Was he running from the law…or something even worse?

She bit her lip trying to stop the questions raging in her head. Yet, they still came, assaulting her with so many different possibilities she was almost afraid to even look at the guy again. The lights still dimly lit the barn. Guess he never got up to turn them off.

Pearl and Josie stuck their heads out for some pets, but she couldn't get any words out for them through her choked throat. She slowly peeked around into the last pen…

Boots, fancy-city boots. Holding her breath, she stood up on her tiptoes to look over the gate. He was definitely still in a deep sleep with his good arm flung over his face and his injured arm snug against his chest. At least she hoped it was just sleep. She set his coffee on the post of the gate before skirting the edge of the pen. She knelt closer to him until she could hear the soft exhale of his breath and see his chest rise and fall.

Goodness, his expansive chest and shoulders looked like they could carry the weight of the world. Her pulse raced as she saw the massive size of his arms and hands, hands that would make hers feel tiny and delicate. For a moment she thought what it would feel like in his arms, safe and protected from the harshness of life.

He stirred, and she hastily crawled back out before he saw her drooling over him. *Get ahold of yourself girl!* She smacked herself on the forehead. Yet, she couldn't stop her mind from retracing the line of his stubbled chin, the expanse of his shoulders...

"Mahhh." Josie nudged her with her muzzle.

"Sorry, girl," she whispered, shaking her head and focusing on her task. She had been alone way too long.

Sydney finished her morning chores, including snatching a half dozen fresh eggs, and headed back to the house to scramble a couple of them up for breakfast. Nothing like fresh eggs. She ate slowly. Something she did her best to do every morning, enjoying the early sing-song of the ranch, real-farm-raised food, and the peace that always filled her when she remembered that this place was hers.

For a moment, she almost forgot about the handsome stranger still asleep in the barn.

The deep rumble of Homer's quad brought her out her stillness. She appreciated that the older man stayed on after Aunty Mag and Uncle Joe passed. His help had kept her afloat, and today it brought her a sense of safety with the man in her barn.

She rose and stretched. Chores still had to be done, handsome stranger or not. She cleaned up breakfast, but then thought of her unexpected guest. Should she make him something to eat?

Not one to lollygag, she quickly heated the pan and cracked a couple more eggs. He needed his strength to decide where in the world he would go now, being as he had no memory. What would he do? She couldn't just send him off hurt and with no memory, could she? The thought plagued her as she pushed through her screen with a plate of eggs in one hand.

Just as the screen door slammed shut, the yelling in the barn began. Guardian ran ahead of her as she did her best to run without spilling the food.

~*~

A kick shook him again. Pain lanced through his sleep mussed brain, kicking in his instincts. Without thought, he jumped towards the man who kicked him. He took the man's fist and twisted it behind his back.

The man grunted as his weathered face twisted in pain.

A massive white dog came running towards them, growling in threat.

"No, let him go!" a woman yelled as she ran toward him with a plate of food in one hand.

His mind swirled, memories fighting to force their way to the surface. He blinked his eyes several times before finally focusing on the fierce multi-colored eyes of the woman in front of him. His brow furrowed, and slowly he relaxed just a tad.

"Sydney." His voice crackled as he blinked his eyes rapidly.

"Yes, that's me. Please let Homer go." Her soft voice soothed the shaking inside of him. She held his gaze and walked slowly, calmly towards them.

"You know him?" he asked her.

"I'm the foreman," Homer's raspy voice shot out gruffly.

He looked to Sydney. She nodded. He gently released the older man, never letting go of her gaze.

"What…" he started and shook his head before grasping the stall gate for support.

"You leave your date to sleep in the barn, Syd?" The foreman rubbed his arm, watching him as he backed into the stall.

"He's not my date." The blush that crept across her cheeks faded her freckles, and he couldn't take his eyes off her even with nothing making sense at the moment.

"Oh, you already found my replacement? I have until

21

June, ya know. My son could do without me until August if absolutely necessary." The older man kicked at the straw at his feet.

"I know, Homer. I appreciate you staying this long even though you planned to retire last year." Sydney set down the plate, walked over to the older man, and checked his arm.

"It's fine," the foreman said gruffly before he turned and hobbled out with the tools he had come in to fetch.

Sydney watched him until he disappeared out the barn door.

"Replacement?" he said in a halting voice. He had watched the interaction, doing his best to piece together what was happening.

Sydney turned quickly toward him. He had lost most of the daze that had ahold of him just moments before. Sleep slowly faded away, yet his brain still buzzed with a strange emptiness.

"Yeah," she said, watching him intensely. "Why did you grab Homer like that? He's no threat."

"I, uh." He looked down at his feet. "It was pure reaction."

"Still no memory?" she sighed.

"No."

She handed him the plate from where she had set it on the fence post. He looked at her as he took it and gave her a slight smile. Did her gaze just soften slightly?

The smell of the food in his hands distracted him. Without preamble, he inhaled the breakfast she had brought.

Sydney leaned against the fence and watched him. When he finished, he handed her the plate with a sheepish grin.

"Thank you, I was hungry." He cleared his throat. "I would say those were the best eggs I've ever had, but I guess I don't really know."

"Have you thought about what you are going to do?"

she asked him, her eyes seeming like she actually cared.

"No, ma'am. I truthfully haven't had the chance. Exhaustion overtook me." As his situation came back to him in full force, that buzzing anxiety flared inside of him again.

"I could still call Wil…I mean Sheriff Whitmore."

He cocked his head and watched her. By her comment he knew that this sheriff was more than just law enforcement to her. Watching her freckles fade in her blush confirmed his suspicion. "He a friend of yours?"

"No. Yes." She blew out a breath. "He kind of used to be. It's a small town."

"I see." He continued to watch her. "Do you trust him?"

"No." The word exited her quickly, and she threw a hand over her mouth.

"That settles it. I would rather you didn't involve him then, if you are comfortable with that?"

She watched him for several moments. Yet, it didn't seem uncomfortable. He knew she needed to feel him out. He wouldn't blame her for not trusting him. He was a stranger, and a stranger with no memory and no idea what trouble he might bring upon her.

"So what are you going to do?" she asked him.

He shifted his weight, the anxiety becoming almost physical. A few deep breaths later, the buzz eased and he felt confident in his own skin again. He had no idea what past he had come from or what he would do for the future since he had no idea of even his name. Though, he knew he could work and hold his own, even as banged up as he was.

"Well, I heard you need a replacement." He looked at her from under his arched brows.

"I, uh…" She hesitated, looking from him to the barn door and back again.

"At least until I remember something? I'll sleep out here. I won't bother you, and I'll do whatever I can to help." Somehow it felt right to be here. This woman had opened her barn up to him and helped calm the anxiety of not knowing, well, anything.

"Do you know anything about goats?" She cocked her head to the side, and he couldn't help the softening he felt inside of him for her.

"I don't remember anything right now, Ma'am. Looking at these hands, though, I would say I know how to work." He held his massive paws up, and he caught her licking her lips. Putting his hands back down caused him to grimace, and he pulled his arm closer to his chest again.

"Let me have a look at that shoulder." She took two steps over to him and slid her hands up his arm and around his shoulder.

Heat filled his body instantly, awakening a part of him that was definitely not lost. *Focus, you have nothing to offer this lady.* He took in a deep breath and with it came the smell of her—sweet and pleasant.

She pushed gently around his shoulder, and he took in a sharp breath. "Can you feel this?" She traced her finger down the inside of his palm to his finger tip.

"Definitely," he breathed out as her touch left a trail of fire that seemed to consume him. "You a doctor or something?" he asked to distract himself.

"No, but I know dislocated shoulders." Her eyes were focused and her voice had taken on a professional tone.

He twisted to see her, a question in his eyes.

"Swimming." She shrugged. "I used to be a swimmer."

He nodded and grimaced. "The pain seems familiar, so it probably isn't the first time I've done it. You know how to put it back in?"

"Yeah, but you should probably let a doctor do it."

"Ain't gonna happen." He braced his legs. "How do you want me?"

A small smile curved up the corners of her mouth, and she turned quickly to hide it.

Heat filled him, distracting him from the pain he knew

24

would come.

"On your back," she said, a bit abruptly. "It's going to hurt like the dickens."

"Figured." He blew out his breath as he lay back on the makeshift bed. "Do it."

Quickly, as if she were afraid she might change her mind, she gently pulled his arm alongside him and bent his elbow so his hand pointed towards the roof. With increasing, but tender, tension she pulled his arm down. Soon it popped back into place with a sickening smacking thump. He sucked in a sharp breath and ground his teeth, but he uttered no sound. Her grip and strength surprised him, and he tried to focus on that rather than the pain that lanced through him.

"Better?" she asked as she laid his arm back on his chest.

He rose and moved around a little. His arm, though sore, felt a million times better. "Yeah. Yeah, it is!" He squeezed her shoulder with a full smile. "Thank you."

"No problem." She looked at him, really seemed to take him in and read his eyes.

He hoped she saw the truth, that she could trust him.

She disappeared for a moment and then returned with a cloth. Without asking, she wrapped his arm in sling-like fashion and stood back.

"I will need a fully functional replacement." She crossed her arms across her chest. For being such a slight woman, her movements held strength.

"Really?" he asked, feeling the right side of his mouth turning up.

"Trial basis only. I will call Sheriff Whitmore the second I feel something not right."

"Deal." He nodded.

"What else is injured? Let's have a look at that head." She spent the next several minutes checking his injuries.

His head was actually not as bad as he had originally feared. The leg that he hobbled on last night seemed to be able to bend this morning, yet it pained him. He had probably twisted his knee. He had road rash in multiple places on his arms, back, and it felt like on his legs and hips, but he hadn't had the chance to inspect those.

"You should clean these abrasions out." She sized him up again. "I'll show you to the bathroom."

He followed her towards the house in shock that she would allow him to invade her space. He could be a criminal escaping the law. He could be a psycho, but he didn't think so. She had no idea though. Either she was naïve, trusting, or she felt the undercurrent between them as much as he did.

"I do appreciate this, Sydney." He kept his voice calm, hoping she could hear his gratitude. Things could have gone really badly had she called her sheriff friend.

"Just don't make me regret it." She threw the words over her shoulder.

A smile warmed through him. He liked her spunk.

At the door, he took off his boots and put them to the side on the porch. Whoever he was, he had manners that had been ingrained in him.

"Bathroom is the first door on the left. Towels are in the cupboard. I'm going to try to find you some clothes." She turned away and headed back outside.

The basic bathroom didn't have a counter full of makeup or a blow dryer and curling iron. A peek in the shower showed simple shampoo and a bar of soap. It could be just a guest bathroom, but it smelled like her so he didn't think so. The older, small home probably only had the one bathroom. Although there wasn't an overall female presence to the room, there also was no sign of a male presence.

No boots were outside, no sign of other vehicles to show someone else lived here and was just gone. This woman really did run this ranch on her own. Well, and the man whose arm he had almost ripped off. What was his name? Homer. Yes, he seemed like a decent guy though.

He didn't whine about the mistake.

He took off the sling and grunted as he pulled his tattered shirt over his head and injured shoulder. It proved to be a difficult feat. Road rash lined his side and back. Removing his ripped pants showed more along the left side of his thigh as well. Bruising discolored a good part of him, his chest and stomach, arms, and the left side of his body. He was a mess.

The hot water felt good even as it stung his abrasions. His muscles began to relax as he stood under the stream. He took in a haggard breath. What had happened to him? Who was he? Not knowing these most vital answers left an uneasy quelling inside of him.

A soft knock on the door woke him from his perplexing.

"I found some clothes that might fit," Sydney said through the door.

His heart thundered as he heard the door slowly open. Was she really coming in here? He peeked around the shower curtain, sure to keep his lower half hidden behind it.

Sydney set a stack of clothes on the counter. Their eyes locked for a moment, before hers traveled down his chest and then raced back up to meet his gaze.

"Thank you," he said, his voice deeper than normal.

"They were my uncle's, I hope they fit. Okay, uh, enjoy the rest of the shower." Her voice quivered slightly, and she hastily slipped back out into the hallway.

He stared at the door for a second more before dropping the curtain and returning to his shower. No longer did he stress over who he was or what had happened. The only thoughts that stayed active in his mind involved multi-colored eyes and freckled cheeks washing out under the pink of her blush.

# ~3~

Sydney stopped struggling with the wire on the chicken coop for a moment to soak in the warm sun topping over the trees. She breathed in the fresh scent of new life, budding leaves and grass sprouts, and the beginnings of blossoms opening on the fruit trees.

Guardian, who lay close by, lifted his head and let out a low woof.

She followed the dog's gaze to the stranger exiting her house. Biting her lips, she swallowed the giggle that wanted to burst forth. Guess the no-name cowboy was bigger than her uncle. He walked uncomfortably in high water jeans and a t-shirt that looked like it was painted on.

As funny as it was, her breath caught as he closed the distance between them because she could see how the shirt hugged each perfectly sculpted peck and his washboard stomach.

"A little tight," he said with a shrug, letting the one-sided smile cross his lips. His limp was barely discernible now. She should have checked out his knee too.

"Yeah, just a little." She did her best to avert her eyes, and Homer rounding the corner gave her the perfect escape.

"Hey Syd, I...what in the world, man? You let her do your laundry? This girl didn't catch that gene."

Sydney's face flushed, and she busied herself with the stubborn wire on the coop. Homer was right though, it wouldn't have been the first batch of clothes she had ruined.

"I'm headed into town for supplies. Want me to pick up some clothes to replace those?" Homer asked.

"That's actually a great idea, Homer. Thank you. Just put them on the ranch's tab." Relief flooded Sydney with a way to sidestep the embarrassment.

"What are you, Hotshot, an extra-large? And definitely a thirty-six in length, not a thirty-two." Homer wheezed out a chuckle.

She couldn't help but smile. It had been awhile since she had heard the older man laugh.

"Sounds about right, sir. Thank you." The cowboy sounded gracious, but he pushed back his shoulders as much as he could with being injured. Must be hard on the man's ego to accept gifts.

"Oh, it's sir now...?" Homer turned, mumbling to himself.

"Oh, and a hat. Yeah, a wide brim," Sydney called after him.

The older man nodded and walked out to the ranch truck.

"I can't thank you enough," No-Name said, locking onto her gaze with those dazzling green eyes of his. "I'll make it square as soon as I figure what's going on."

"I'll take it out of your pay." She shrugged and focused on her task.

"Good deal." He nodded. "I'm going to walk back out to the road to look for evidence where I, uh, woke up last night. Now that it's light I might be able to see something."

"Do you ride?" She smacked her forehead. "Sorry, would you like to ride? The horses need exercise."

"I would, but..." He pointed to his shoulder.

"Yeah, so that's twice I wish I could put my foot in my mouth." She shook her head and dropped the wire she had been messing with. "By the way, where is the sling?"

"I couldn't get it back on." He pulled the fabric from where he had tucked it into his back pocket.

"Come on. I'll fix up the sling, and then we'll take my truck."

"I don't want to keep you from your duties."

She laughed. "It's my ranch, and I decide when to do my *duties*. Do you want a ride or not? As you said last night, it's quite the driveway."

"If you're sure. Thank you."

She wrapped the sling around him again, doing her best not to let his clean scent intoxicate her. Every time her hands brushed against his hard chest, fire sparked through her. By the time she finished situating the sling to support his shoulder, her breath came in quick bursts. Before he noticed, she took off at a brisk walk towards the truck.

They hopped into the truck and bounced down the gravel drive. She wondered what it felt like to not remember anything, not have an identity, a history, even a name. This guy took it all so coolly. There were some days she wouldn't have minded losing her memory. Yet, she thought of all the happy moments she had here on the ranch as a child…no, she would never want to lose that.

At the crossroads to the highway, she stopped the truck. Last night he had said he which way he came from, but she couldn't remember.

"Left," he said simply, a small smile in his voice.

"So, I'm directionally challenged." She shrugged.

"I didn't say a thing." Though the smile on his lips said enough.

"Just tell me where to pull over."

"Slow down." He leaned past her scrutinizing the road. "Keep going."

She could smell her shampoo in his hair. It mixed with his own scent and formed an aroma that had her squirming in the seat. His large hand held the dash in front of her as he leaned over to look out the window. *Watch the road, Sydney.*

"Here," he said, throwing the door open and jumping from the still-in-motion truck.

Sydney pulled over in the gravel and put the truck in park.

He crossed the road and walked up and down, and then bent to touch some dark skid marks. He pushed through the gravel on the side of the road, fingered a section where bare ground showed through. Standing back up, he looked up the road, the way they had been headed, towards town. Then he turned back to the marks and followed them in to the trees.

Sydney jumped out of the truck and crossed the road to join him. Keeping out of his way, she stood back and just watched. He was focused, checking broken branches and smudges in the dirt that could be footprints. He didn't seem to miss any detail, and didn't seem to be hampered doing this with one arm in a sling. He headed off further into the forest. A couple minutes later he returned with a torn and smashed, black hat. Her heart raced…*and a cowboy hat.*

"I would say this was probably mine." He inspected the lost hat.

"You seem to know how to track. Think you're a hunter or something?"

He shrugged, carefully punched the hat with his good arm in attempt to straighten it back out, and looked up and down the road again. "It looks like the subject pulled into this area without really slowing down and tossed me out of a truck, I would say, from the distance where I landed from the tire marks."

"The subject? You deducted all of that from little smudges on the ground?"

He shrugged again.

"You a cop?"

His eyes shot to her. "You think so?"

"Most people don't say things like *subject* and can read signs like that." She looked back up the road and to the marks on the ground. "What kind of trouble are you in?"

"I don't know…"

After Homer returned, and the nameless cowboy got

into clothes that fit him much better, Sydney had him follow Homer around for the rest of the day. She kept herself busy with checking on the mama goats who had already had their babies. She kept them in the pen next to the barn. The three kids had already outgrown their wobbly legs. She stroked one of them while amazement washed over her. Such little miracles.

Her mind floated back to the early morning they had been born. The spring storm had whipped through the cracks in the barn, and the whistling sound it made caused the hair on her arms to stand on end. She stayed with them through the night as they labored. When Homer arrived at his usual time that morning, relief washed over her for the two mamas finally began pushing their babies out, both at the same time.

Watching the kids being born had always fascinated Sydney. Even first time mamas seemed to know exactly what to do, how and when to push, how to coddle and lick their babies after birth, how to feed them and nurture them as they grew. The one she helped birth, Sierra, had twins—two boys.

She playfully nuzzled one of them before its brother rammed into him, and the two pounced away. She didn't name the boys. Those were the ones she had to sell. Every few years Uncle Joe would pick one of the males to liven up the breeding stock, but her breeding males were doing just fine right now. Her heart squeezed before pulling away from the playful kids to focus her attention on the milking pen.

"Maah," the tan-colored goat bleated as Sydney neared the pen with the milking goats.

"Yes, Faun. I know you are full. I'm coming." She let her nuzzle under her arm as she opened the gate.

Warmth filled her while she hugged the goat. These animals had become her solace, both as a young girl and now. She shook her head. Never had she thought she would have been lucky enough to have the life she did.

Faun happily munched on the oats while Sydney tugged on her teats in a rhythmic motion. She smiled remembering when her hands used to cramp and scream. Now the repetitive motion only soothed her.

The milk pail slowly filled with each squirt.

She thought about how she would use this particular pail of milk. After finally perfecting the cheese making process last year, she now sold goat cheese locally in the town's grocer and at the farmer's market. In fact, the Mountain Valley Farm Day was coming up in a few months. It was one of her biggest sales days. Between the cheese sales and selling off the males, she made a pretty decent living. Enough to pay off the yearly property taxes and live on for sure, and that was all she needed.

~*~

Homer didn't talk much. Which was fine by him. The cowboy had plenty to think about, and found he didn't fancy himself a talker either. With a few simple instructions, the older man would leave him to finish a task. Some things really pulled on his shoulder and kneeling to mend the fences was quite awkward with his gimpy leg, but there was no way he would complain.

He knew he was lucky to find someone to give him a place to stay while he figured out what to do. Normally the first thing to do in his situation would be to call local law enforcement, yet he couldn't shake the foreboding feeling that overwhelmed him every time he thought of it. Something didn't feel right.

He stood from the last fence post and stretched, scanning the land around him as he did. When his eyes fell on Sydney playing with the goats in a pen, he couldn't look away. Something about that woman pulled him in and made him forget that he was a nameless man in probably a boat load of trouble. He had no right to even have a thought about her, yet he couldn't stop them.

"Hotshot!" Homer yelled from the water trough he struggled to fix.

He nodded and headed towards the older man who eyed him with a sharp, distrustful gaze.

"You here to work or to ogle?" Homer asked him as he came alongside the trough.

He gave the older man a sharp glare as he bristled inside and his fists clenched. Being talked to like this felt foreign, and it did not set well with him.

"That girl there needs someone she can rely on. Now, if you're ready to work, you have a lot to learn. Starting with lifting this and scrubbing out the bottom."

Though he seethed, the man knew it best to keep his mouth shut. Besides, the foreman was right. How would he treat a man showing up out of nowhere to take over his position? Especially a man who couldn't keep his eyes off the pretty boss.

~*~

Sydney was brushing Guardian when Homer started up his quad and waved farewell. As he left a trail of dust down the drive to his place, she glanced at Nameless. He scanned the woods around the clearing, the house, and the barn before looking towards her. What was she going to do with this stranger?

He took off his hat as he joined her on the porch.

"That's a lot of fur," he said as she pulled another handful of white hair from the brush.

"Yes, it is." She laughed. "Shedding season is not a clean time around here—one reason why he's an outside dog."

"I saw another one like him out in the field."

"You're observant. That's Thor. He's the goat protector. He stays with the herd." She scratched the dog's exposed belly as his tongue hung out in pleasure. "Guardian here, he took a liking to me and never left my side. Hence the name."

"You always lived out here?"

She gazed up at him. Was he trying to be pleasant or did he really want to know? His green eyes found hers and held on tight. He looked as if she were a puzzle to figure out.

"No, this was my Aunt and Uncle's ranch." She sat up and stretched her back. Guardian took the chance to move further away from the brush. "I spent summers here as a kid. When they...when they passed on, they left it to me."

"I'm sorry." His voice sounded sincere, nothing like the men from her past...*focus, girl.*

"Me too." She cleared her throat and gathered up the large mass of fur. "Need a pillow tonight?"

"I'll pass," he said with a laugh. It was the first real laugh she heard from him, a pleasant, deep rumbling.

"Suit yourself." She shrugged. "Bet it would be softer than that straw."

"It actually wasn't that bad."

Her eyes narrowed. "I don't think you actually felt much last night."

"Could be."

"I'm going to make some dinner. You eat pork chops?" She caught his blank stare. "Ugh, sorry." Would she ever remember not to ask him questions he doesn't have answers to? She rose to go inside, leaving him shifting his weight on the porch. "You might as well come in."

"If you're sure." He took off his boots and followed her into the house, looking around the small space.

"It's not much, but it's home."

"It's perfect," he said, touching little photos hanging on the walls. "This your aunt and uncle?" His thick finger brushed her favorite picture and it came loose. He fumbled it a few times before it finally crashed to the wood floor, glass shattering. "Blast it, Jameson!" He quickly began carefully picking up all the glass.

Sydney rushed over and tried to put the frame back together. Tears threatened and she blinked to keep them back. The photo was unharmed, and she brought it gingerly to her. The frame on the other hand was irreparable.

"I'm sorry, Sydney." His piercing eyes met hers over the mess.

Knowing the picture was undamaged helped ease the loss of the frame. Frames could be replaced. As she looked in his eyes though, his words finally processed through.

"Did you hear what you said?" she asked.

"Yeah, sorry if that word offends you. I will do my best to refrain from it in the future."

"No, not that word. You said, *Jameson.*"

"I did, yes," he said as he eased back, sitting on the floor, his injured leg stretched out awkwardly. "Jameson." He met her eyes with a wide smile. "I have a name!"

"Well, it's nice to finally meet you, Jameson!" She held her hand out to be engulfed by his massive one. A surge of tingly warmth shot through her, and she found herself wishing her hand would stay hidden in his much longer than it did.

The memory of his name seemed to ease Jameson. His shoulders relaxed and his movements had more fluidity rather than rigidness. He didn't stand quite so tight, and he even laughed easily throughout dinner. It sure helped knowing how to address him. *Hey you, Handsome Stranger, or Nameless* just never seemed acceptable.

They kept a light conversation going, mostly about the ranch and the animals. Sydney never knew how difficult small talk could be with someone who had no memory. At a lull in the conversation, she realized the weirdness of this situation. She had cooked dinner for a man that arrived at her doorstep with no memory and a severely bruised and banged up body. Then, a question came to mind that pulled her in. It shot out of her mouth before she had time to think better.

"Jameson—"

"It's so good to have a name again." He smiled and sat back in his chair.

"Why haven't you asked about a husband?" Sydney waited for several moments, watching him, wondering if he would just ignore the question that caused her cheeks to burn slightly.

"Why do you ask?" Jameson did his best to keep his mouth tight, but the corner twitched.

"That's everyone's first question."

"Everyone's?" He leaned forward, resting his one good elbow on the table.

"Yeah, nosy neighbors, delivery people, vets, cops, anyone who comes by really."

"Huh."

"Guess no one thinks a woman can run a ranch without a husband. Though I would have a hard time doing it without Homer." She met his eyes and realized they held an intensity that she didn't quite understand. Her heart quickened and she fiddled with a fork. "Are you going to answer my question?"

"Do you really want to know?" His tone had evened out, becoming almost official.

"Yes."

"When I arrived late last night, your house was quiet besides your sweet voice, talking to yourself or to your animals." He reached down and stroked Mr. Paws who sat on the chair between them. "The tire tracks on your driveway matched the old truck's at the barn. The single, dusty car in your carport hadn't moved since the last rain."

"But that could mean anything. I don't drive my car much anymore. My husband could have been asleep or out."

"The boots by the door were too small to be a man's. The spot next to them was clean, no evidence that there ever had been boots there at all. You came out, with a gun cocked and ready, looking able to do what was necessary to defend your land—and yourself." He shrugged and sat back again. "Plus, you have no ring on your finger nor indentation of one ever being there, and Homer confirmed it today."

"Who are you, Sherlock?" Her lips creased even though

she fought to keep the smile at bay. "You sure you're not a cop?"

"I'm not sure about anything, Syd." The nickname came out smoothly, as if he had called her that for years.

~*~

I have a name. That one amazing thought played over and over as he lay on his bed made from hay. Even with the scent of animal, his makeshift quarters actually suited him just fine. Sure, a bed would be nice, but this beat wandering around, trying to figure out who he was and where to go. At least here, he had purpose, something to keep him busy throughout the day.

Having a name eased so much of his tension. If he remembered that, then surely more would come. He loved that Sydney had caught it. If things had been different, he might have just kissed her then. Knowing his name, though, did not mean he had earned the right to want more from the gracious woman. Besides, they had just met.

He shook his head.

He didn't need to be thinking of the woman who had given him refuge. He needed to be devising a plan to figure out his next steps. It's not like he could just live here forever, hiding away from whatever his past may hold. Yet, that prospect didn't sound too bad...

# ~4~

The next morning, Sydney found Jameson already awkwardly mucking out Pearl and Josie's stalls when she brought coffee to the barn. He kept his left arm tucked in the sling and used only his hand to steady the pitch fork while his right side did most the work. *Doesn't seem to mind hard work.* She shook her head before clearing her throat to announce her presence, though he didn't seem surprised.

"Good morning, Syd." He shoveled out the last bit of soiled hay before leaning on the tool like he had been doing this his whole life.

"Morning, Jameson." She handed him a mug.

He set the shovel against the rails. "I don't think I will ever get tired of hearing my name." The right side of his mouth raised as his fingers briefly touched hers while taking the cup.

Warm tingling shot through her, settling in her stomach. It's just because he's a man. How long had it been since she had spent time around a man besides Homer, especially such a strong, handsome one? Almost two years? That's if she didn't account for Wil's advances. She shook her head to rid herself of the memory.

"You like it black?" she asked to distract herself.

He took a sip. "Seems good, almost like a pleasant memory." His eyes unfocused for a moment before narrowing.

"Something?" she asked, holding her breath.

"Fleeting only. Flashes, but nothing I can hold on to."

"That must be really frustrating." Empathy surged in her.

He shrugged and stood tall. "So, what now?"

His quick change of subject and demeanor threw her for a moment. "Feeding the penned goats, horses, and chickens, collecting eggs, and then breakfast. Then the day really begins."

"Every day?" he asked.

"Every day, rain or shine, sleet or snow, though hail is the worst." She shook her hand, remembering the pain of the last hail storm. Ice chunks almost as big as golf balls came down, leaving her bruised and swollen. One had hit the back of her hand so hard she feared it had been broken for several days before the swelling finally went down.

"You're hardcore, aren't you?"

A full out laugh burst from her. She couldn't hold back the continual force as she laughed like she hadn't in years. After wiping the tears from her eyes and taking a deep breath, she finally met his amused gaze.

They worked the morning chores together, and an easiness settled between them. Sydney hadn't felt this comfortable with a man since, well, not ever. Uncle Joe and she had a relaxed working partnership, but she couldn't compare the man next to her to him. No, the feelings Jameson evoked could never be compared to Uncle Joe.

~*~

Jameson couldn't keep his eyes off of Sydney as she talked him through all the morning chores. Without knowing what his past held, it was hard to say, but he felt like she was different than any other woman he had ever known.

When he had grasped her hand earlier, he noticed the strong grip and roughness of her hands. It hadn't turned him off. More like it affirmed the hard worker she portrayed herself as. She definitely had feminine qualities. In fact, she moved with a grace and sureness that left him helpless to turn away.

He did his best to pay attention to her directions so that he could do most of the chores the following morning. Her soft voice, though, held him in a trance, and all he wanted to do was become lost in it.

It would feel better lost in her, than lost in the wanderings of his mind. Was anyone looking for him or missing him? More than likely he had family somewhere, a job, someone out there that had noticed he had disappeared. Would they find him here, on a goat ranch in the middle of nowhere?

Sydney drew his attention back to the tasks at hand. Part of him wasn't sure he wanted anyone to find him. He continued to watch all Sydney did, memorizing her movements and the graceful way she moved even in the midst of chores that required a tough strength.

~*~

Sydney walked to the house for breakfast in an effortless discussion with Jameson of the difference between store-bought eggs and fresh-out-of-the-coop eggs. As they entered, her eyes strayed to the missing picture of Aunty Mag and Uncle Joe. Her routine had a missing piece that left a tightness in her heart. She had paused just a fraction of a moment, but Jameson ground his teeth and his body slightly tensed.

"Anyway," she said to relieve the tension while rinsing the eggs in the sink. "I don't have a store bought egg to compare, but farm fresh eggs are brighter. When you scramble them, they are more yellow than store bought eggs. They taste better, and they're more nutritious, especially since most of these are fertilized eggs."

"Fertilized?" He sat at the table at the end of the small kitchen.

Having a small house had its perks. It meant she could easily have a conversation even if the other person sat in a different room.

"Yeah, you know, like the birds and the bees," she teased.

He furrowed his brow and shrugged his shoulders.

"The rooster did his part," she said and glanced at his

blank stare. "If left alone, this egg would have turned into a chick."

His face paled. "You mean we're eating a chick fetus?"

"Ugh, I can't think of it that way." She shook her head. "Just know that it tastes better and is better for you. Let's just leave it at that."

Memories of Aunty Mag trying to explain the same thing to her as a young girl filtered through. She hadn't eaten eggs for the rest of that summer. To this day, if she thought too much of where all of her food came from, she could lose her appetite. In the end she knew it was more nutritious, and she had notice a remarkable difference in her health.

She snuck a glance at Jameson while cracking the first egg into the pan. His nose crinkled. She had planned to cook fried eggs this morning, but instead she grabbed the spatula and started scrambling the yolk with the tiny red dot showing the sign of fertilization.

She pulled out a paper wrapped slab of ham and diced some up before tossing them into the pan along with the eggs.

"Do you get that ham from the butcher?" he asked, nodding towards the paper.

"Oh, uh, no. I have neighbor that I trade with. Every year they get a goat, and I get a half a hog. They butcher their animals themselves."

"Huh." He sat back in his chair and watched her silently.

She washed some peppers, mushrooms, and spinach, but as she began chopping the vegetables, a thought struck her. Many men she knew didn't like vegetables. "Do you like veggies—ugh, I'm sorry." She slapped her forehead as regret sat heavy in her belly.

"Yes," he answered quickly.

Her eyes snapped back to him. "Yes?" she asked.

"It came out instantly. It seems correct."

Sydney tore her eyes away from his endearing grin and

did her best to focus on chopping. Yet, she couldn't concentrate and kept looking over to the stranger who didn't feel so strange anymore.

"Ouch!" she cried out, instantly shoving her finger into her mouth.

Jameson was on his feet and to her before she even had an idea of what had happened.

"You okay?" he asked as he gently took her finger from out of her mouth.

"Yeah, just a little cut," she said, not knowing how to respond to his proximity or his concern. His hand holding hers faded any pain she had away like a fresh spring breeze. Little drops of blood began beading on her finger. "I...I'll just go get a band aid. Could you please keep an eye on breakfast for me? I don't want it to burn."

"Uh, sure," he said, though his voice sounded anything but sure. His eyes scanned between the cutting board and the pan on the stove.

Sydney quickly made her escape, trying to catch her breath while doing so. Her hand still tingled from where he had held it. Why did she always go for the bad boys? This guy didn't even have a memory of how bad he actually was. He had nice manners, but she could feel it in her blood—he was a bad boy. Besides, nice guys don't get left beaten in the middle of the road.

The cut stung as she rinsed it off in the sink. She then held it tight with a tissue to stop the bleeding. Why did he have to show more concern than number one or number two? A small smile tugged at her mouth in memory of her friend making fun of her. She had replied to her, *Yes, I numbered my exes. It's better than saying their names and all the emotion wrapped up in them.* Her friend had never bothered her about calling her exes by numbers again.

Why did she compare them to Jameson anyway? Was she really that desperate for male company? All any man had done was cause her heartache and memories she wished she could bury. She didn't want to go through all that again, even for a tall, dark, handsome stranger with magnificent green eyes and large hands. Yet, she had wished for that, hadn't she. Might Jameson be worth a chance to try again?

"Meow," sounded with a scratch at the door. Saved by that cat. She opened the door and gave a few pets to the furry feline before she heard murmured curses from the kitchen. She strode down the hall to investigate with her heart pounding.

She had only been gone a matter of moments but it looked like a tornado had landed in the kitchen. Vegetables looked hacked and destroyed all over the counter. Eggs had splattered out of the pan all over the stove. Coffee had spilled and been half cleaned with the rag still sitting in the puddle. Her mouth dropped, but when Jameson looked over with a sheepish, half-proud smile, she couldn't keep the laughter from bubbling forth.

"Well, I guess we know you aren't a cook," she teased while taking the spatula from his hand.

"Here I thought I was doing a bang-up job." His lower lip protruded slightly and urges she hadn't felt in years sprang forth.

Luckily the pan's popping and sizzling woke her up from this *playing-house* moment. *Sydney, you are losing it girl.* Her heart hammered loudly while she did her best to focus on salvaging what she could of their breakfast.

Jameson cleaned up the rest of the spilled coffee and wrung the dish cloth out in the sink. Then he relaxed in the chair again, watching her.

"So, I guess I need to work on my cooking skills." He chuckled lightly. "That's not too bad of a flaw is it?"

"No." She laughed, thinking he did more than most men. In fact, she hadn't experienced even one who had ever attempted to cook a meal that didn't involve opening a can or using the microwave. "It was a good try."

"Hey, I could learn."

Her hand paused in the air, and she turned to face his

brilliant green eyes. "You know, I think you actually could."

While they ate, she noticed Jameson scratching at his stubbled face with his thick fingers. He looked rugged with the starting of a beard, and maybe even a little more handsome. It obviously irritated him though.

"I don't think you're used to two days without shaving."

He dropped his hand, but then immediately reached up to feel the bristly hair. "Yeah, I would gather not."

"Would you like to use a razor?"

"No offense, Syd, but I doubt your lady blades would do much on this thick stubble."

She shrugged.

"Maybe I'll let it grow…" His eyes faded just as his voice did, and she wondered if he searched his missing memory for something.

They continued to eat in silence. Sydney sensed he needed his space. It would be difficult to not constantly be thinking of what you didn't know and what you should know. She chuffed lightly, thinking of all the things she would be happy to forget. Then her eyes caught the worn wooden table, the nicked chairs, the sun-faded curtains, and memories of happy summers consumed her. No, she wouldn't want to forget those.

# ~5~

Jameson's frustration grew as Homer repeated the same words he had for what seemed like the hundredth time. He felt like he was a quick study, so why did trimming goats' hooves sound like a foreign language to him. It didn't help that he had felt preoccupied all morning.

Between a gnawing sense that something or someone was coming for him and not being able to keep his eyes off his new boss, it was a wonder he could concentrate at all. He scanned the tree line again.

"Hello, are you in there, Hotshot? How do expect to take care of Miss Sydney when you can't focus enough to learn how to trim these hooves?"

How could he expect to take care of Syd? With no memory and sure that trouble waited for him, he knew he was no good for her. An incessant tugging resounded in him, urging him to flee before that trouble found him and put Syd in harm's way. His eyes found her again. He had no desire to leave her.

The older man cleared his throat and looked pointedly at him.

With a deep breath, he forced himself to pay attention to the man and learn how to accomplish the task that he could handle right now. This he could do. Everything else, he had no idea how to proceed.

~*~

Sydney's gaze strayed to where Homer instructed Jameson. She tried to focus on Olive, the goat it was taking her forever to milk. The animal looked back at her and bleated.

"I know girl, I'm sorry. I'll focus." It took physical effort to do so, but she finished the milking and sent the goat off with the rest of the milking herd. She stretched her hands and her back before hauling the full bucket back to the barn.

Right before she walked out of sight, she stole one more glimpse of Jameson. This time though, his intense green eyes connected with hers. She tripped over a divot in the dirt and barely caught herself before the milk pail turned over. He didn't see that, did he?

A quick glance showed his hastily averted eyes and a small sideways grin that he did his best to hide. He saw.

She chastised herself the whole time she processed the milk. She would have enough extra that would age in time for Mountain Valley Farm Day.

She was still processing cheese when she heard the rumble of Homer's quad take off down the dirt road that led to his place. Only moments later she sensed the larger than life presence of Jameson in the doorway. His scent carried on a breeze from the open door, causing her knees to quiver. *Focus girl.*

"There you are," his deep voice flowed out.

She nodded, not trusting herself to not blurt out something stupid.

He leaned back on the doorframe. He was the picture of the sexy cowboy. All he needed to do was take off his shirt, and he would fit on one of those steamy romance books perfectly.

"I gather this is the cheese-making room?" He scanned the cheeses in various stages strung up throughout the small room.

"Yep," she breathed out. *Single words answers, I got this. Just don't come any closer.*

He uncrossed his arms and slowly made his way to her. Had he heard her? Her heartbeat drowned out all the other sounds and her hands shook. She kneaded the cheese with more vigor to cover up the wavering.

"Do you need help with this?" He stood so close behind her that the breath of his words caressed her neck, causing a few tendrils of hair that escaped her bun to blow in its breeze.

"Nope," she quickly chirped out. Knead, roll, knead, focus.

"Well, then," he scooted around to the side of her, scratched his chin, and pushed his hat further back on his head. "If you don't mind, I would love to use your shower."

"Sure." Yeah, that's right, Sydney. One word answers, breathe.

He watched her for a few more moments, eyebrows furrowed. Then he turned and left the room.

Finally she could breathe again, but it took another ten minutes for her heart to slow to a less deafening roar. What was she going to do with this man working so close with her? Whether she was falling for him, or if it was because a lack of male attention for too long, she couldn't seem to control her body whenever he got near. Well, not even when he was in her line of sight.

~*~

The sun greeted Jameson with filtered rays skimming over the top of the regal pines. He took a minute to breath in the fresh spring air. This piece of property was a dream—mostly level land surrounded by a fortress of pines and spruces. The house, though small and older, held a sweet feeling of coming home, just like its owner.

Jameson shook his head as he continued towards the house. The echo of his feet on the porch felt right. In less than forty-eight hours he already was at ease here. He tugged off both muddy boots and left them in the clean spot next to where Sydney kept hers.

Sydney.

His heart felt oddly light and fluttery thinking of her. She kept him on his toes, seeming to state her mind clearly, and yet like she just had a few minutes ago, make him wonder if he imagined the look in her eyes.

She probably just watched him like she did to make sure he didn't steal something or mistreat her animals. She sure seemed to love those creatures, not that they weren't cute in their own way. Watching those babies romp around did put a smile on his face.

The screen slammed behind him, causing him to startle. He was going to have to remember that it closed so aggressively. After a breath to calm his high alert response, his eyes went directly to the empty place on the wall. He still felt horrible for that picture breaking like it did. Sydney did her best to act like it was okay, but it obviously meant a lot to her. He would have to find a way to fix that frame.

"Meow." The cat rubbed against his pants, his purr filling the quiet house.

"Well, hello to you too." Jameson chuckled. He guessed he would talk to animals just like Sydney did if he was alone all the time.

He gave the cat one last scratch on the head, and then strolled into the bathroom. He opened the cupboard where Sydney had cleared out a small shelf for the clothes she had Homer buy him. She really had been a blessing to find. Anyone else probably would have called the Sheriff right away or at the least sent him on his way. Why had she allowed him to stay?

As the room steamed up while the water warmed, Jameson watched his reflection slowly disappear in the condensation on the mirror. He knew his face, his name, and he began to notice what type of man he was, but where had he come from? What was his life like before two days ago? And who in the world beat him up and left him on the side of the road?

The hot water blasted his head as he leaned against the shower wall and let the dirt, grime, and sweat wash off him. He tried to let all the uncertainties follow them down the drain. Yet, even after he dried off and put on a pair of pants, the questions still haunted him.

He wiped the mirror, but it immediately fogged back up. He opened the door and let the cool air rush in and the steam wisp out. Soon the mirror cleared and he leaned forward to look himself in the eye. Maybe if he searched hard enough, he would find himself in there somewhere.

## ~6~

A smile crept across Sydney's face when she saw Jameson's boots by the front door. She pulled hers off and left them in their normal spot right next to his. A tingle shot down her spine. How could something as simple as a pair of boots cause such a reaction?

Entering the house she was greeted by the scent of the humid shower. The steam escaped from the open door. Her heart seized. *Oh my goodness, he didn't shower with the door open, did he?* No water sounded, but the light glowed into the short hallway.

His voice, soft and mumbled, carried to where she stood frozen. No words could be made out really, only the tone. She thought of sneaking closer, but shook her head and turned toward the kitchen to see what dinner options might be. With someone else here, it made her actually cook rather than just grabbing a piece of fruit and some cheese or something. Before she lived here, she would have just poured herself a bowl of cereal. Life had changed drastically over the last almost two years.

For the better.

"Meow."

"Yes, Mr. Paws." She poured some food in his dish. "Here you go."

The cat weaved in and out of her legs a few times before going to munch on his food. Sydney wondered what he and Guardian thought of the intrusion by this stranger.

She needed to change out of her grubby clothes before she started on dinner, but fear rooted her socked feet to the wood floor. What would she see if she walked by that open, steaming door? Her active imagination filled in the blanks and heat burned her cheeks.

With decision she took the meat out of the fridge and added seasoning to it before letting it soak in the marinade. Then she had nothing to keep her busy so she started with purpose towards the bathroom.

"Who are you?" Jameson's tortured voice crossed the distance, clear as day.

She froze. Empathy washed through her and a heaviness landed in the pit of her stomach. Here she was, so worried about what to do with this hot cowboy in her life, and the poor guy struggled with so much more. She turned and tip-toed back outside, ensuring the screen door didn't slam.

Guardian ambled over to her after she sat in the porch swing and positioned himself so she could brush his head with each sway.

"Hey boy," she lamented with him. He nudged up under her arm as much as he could. "Yeah, I know."

"You know what?" Jameson's deep voice startled her.

She instantly stopped her feet from swinging her. His new clothes fit him well, but there was no hiding his wide build or built chest. She wondered if he used to work out.

"Do you always talk to your animals like that?" he asked before relaxing against the railing opposite of her.

"Yeah," she said with a shrug. *Keep the conversation about him, think about what he was going through.* "When you're alone it's nice to have a conversation with someone." She laughed, and he rewarded with his lopsided grin.

"How long have you been...alone?" The way he hesitated made her look closer at him.

"What, now you ask about the man, or absence thereof, in my life?"

"Just a question." He shrugged as if it didn't matter, but the stiffness in his shoulders said something entirely different.

"Almost two years." She met his eyes, and then they

wouldn't let her go.

"That's a long time…to be alone."

"It would be if you liked people." She forced herself to smile. Her statement held some truth, but looking at him, she knew once he remembered who he was and left, that feeling of loneliness would be overpowering. How quickly she had accepted his company.

"You don't like people?" he asked.

"What's with all the questions?" She stood and held her breath as she walked past him to the door. Breathing his scent in this proximity could undo her.

He followed her into the kitchen where she finished the preparations for dinner. She tossed a salad together, wishing he would sit down at the table instead of leaning against the cupboards watching her.

"When you," he started, cleared his throat, and continued, "don't have a memory of your own, memories seem more valuable." He shrugged and crossed his arms across his broad chest. "Maybe listening to some of yours would somehow help me recall some of mine."

A long silence enveloped them. Sydney thought of all the memories she wished would disappear. She didn't want to relieve those, much less share them. Better to stick with the past that brought those feel-good emotions. She wanted to keep conversations around him, but how could she deny his request?

"When I came out here as a kid," she said, and he took a few steps closer to her and resettled himself. His complete attention softened her heart. When was the last time someone really wanted to hear what she had to say? "It felt like freedom."

"Freedom?" His posture tightened.

"Yeah," she said. "It was so peaceful here." A few goats bleated loudly. Perfect timing, she thought with a smile.

"Peaceful, huh?"

"Not necessarily quiet, but peaceful."

He watched her silently, and when she didn't continue, he asked, "What were your aunt and uncle like?"

"Peaceful." She sighed. "They always spoke kindly to and about each other. Their eyes sparkled of love when they retold stories of their younger years. Ranch life is hard work, but they never complained, never got down on one another for not doing enough."

"Sounds like good people."

"Yeah, they were." Her eyes strayed to the photo before remembering it had fallen.

Jameson ground his teeth.

Poor guy was too hard on himself. To distract him, and herself, she picked up the meat and walked out to the porch to start up the barbeque.

"You grill, too?" he asked as he followed her.

"Well, if I want it, I have to do it, ya know."

He sat in a chair and leaned the back against the house.

"Uncle Joe always sat there. We came out here every evening after dinner. As a kid, he would play, *What can you hear?* with me. I learned to recognize the difference between a coyote and a wolf howl. Here on this porch I heard my first grunt of a bear, call of an owl, cry of a fox, and so much more." She let her eyes scan the darkening sky, noticing billowy, forbidding clouds rolling in. "It's amazing how alive this place becomes at night."

The wind whipped up, blowing the loose strands of her hair around. The breeze held the promise of rain, a smell like no other.

"Storm's coming," she said as she plopped the steaks on the grill.

"You a weather forecaster too."

"No, smart-aleck." She pointed at the clouds quickly building in and blocking the light left in the sky. "Look for yourself."

"I know. Just teasing."

"The kids will come tonight."

"You have kids?" He shifted to the edge of the seat.

"No. Pearl and Josie, they will have their babies tonight."

He scratched his chin and shook his head. "A weather forecaster, a griller, and premonitions, now just whose house did I land at?"

"No premonition." She shrugged. "Experience."

"Storms mean baby goats?" he asked jokingly.

"When they are this close, yeah. Don't ask me why. It's just how it is." She flipped the steaks. "We should get to bed early. Once they go into labor there won't be much sleep being had."

His face paled slightly, but he didn't argue with her.

~*~

Jameson walked the perimeter of the main part of the property. Sydney had sent him off to bed, but he knew he wouldn't have been able to fall asleep yet. He couldn't tell if he was excited or nervous about the thought of helping to birth baby goats. He had no idea where he came from, but this did not feel normal.

However, roaming out here in the dark searching for danger, did feel natural and comfortably normal.

He froze as movement shifted in the brush ahead of him. His breath slowed even as his heart rate sped up. Every part of him became alive and alert. When a long-eared rabbit hopped from behind the bush, Jameson smiled. The rabbit twitched its nose and loped off into the woods as the sky lit up for a split second.

Thunder crashed in the distance. Looks like the weather forecaster was right. He ambled past the house on the way to the barn. The bathroom light turned off and a few seconds later the bedroom light turned on. He paused beside a tree, unable to move as he saw her shadow moving.

She seemed so vulnerable, living out here on her own, at the mercy of nature and man. Yet, he smiled as he remembered how she had greeted him. She wasn't as vulnerable as most would suspect.

Before he couldn't, he pushed away from the tree and made his way to the barn. Wouldn't it be funny if in his old life he lived a ritzy existence and now he slept in a barn? It was only temporary, but where would he be without it?

He petted the bleating goats on his way to the last stall. In his straw bed he stretched out, feeling like he lived a dream he would soon wake from to a harsh reality that awaited him.

~*~

Sydney couldn't sleep, again. Every time her mind traveled to Jameson, she redirected it towards sleep. Birthing kids on no sleep was no good. Especially because she expected both goats carried twins. More complications can happen in twin births.

Her will must have worked because she slept hard, so hard that she didn't wake up until a light touch on her shoulder and someone calling her name jarred her awake.

"Syd, Sydney." Jameson shook her a little, his voice frantic.

Sleep kept trying to pull her back in while she pondered why Jameson was in her room. *Wait! Jameson was in her room!* Adrenaline spiked through her.

"What!?" She sat upright and pulled the blankets to cover the thin tank top she slept in.

"I don't know what to do! They sound like they're dying!"

"Oh, the goats." She plopped back against her pillow, a wash of relief soothing the prickles that had shot through her. "How long?"

"Hour or so?" He shifted his weight back and forth.

"There's several more to go." She stole a glance at him as he remained standing there watching her, shadows increasing his look of bewilderment. "Okay, okay, I'll get up."

A held breath escaped him, but he just took a step back and continued watching. His wet shirt clung to him and his hat dripped in a slow, steady rhythm.

"Uh, do you mind?" She nodded towards the door.

"Oh, yeah." His voice sounded flushed, like if the lights had been on, Sydney thought she would have seen a blush covering his dark, stubbled cheeks.

Once she heard him pacing in the living room, she quickly threw on some clothes. She made a mental list of everything she would need: warm water, rags, and gloves.

"Is this really normal?" Jameson asked as soon as she made it to the living room.

Pearl and Josie's desperate bleats carried on the whipping wind. She looked at Jameson. His rain-soaked hair and shirt clung to him and goosebumps rose on his bare barrel-like arms.

"Yes, giving birth is not easy nor pain-free." She grabbed her coat and Uncle Joe's, which hadn't left the hanger for two years. Dust floated off it as she shook it out and handed it to Jameson. "I hope it fits."

He slipped it on, and though snug across the shoulders, it would do for now. He looked to the barn and back to her again. "What can I do?"

~*~

Jameson's eyes frantically shifted from each of the birthing goats to Syd and back to the goats. An unnerving, anxious shaking had begun in him the moment they first woke him up with their frantic bleating. His bewilderment only grew as Sydney reacted calmly, almost slowly. He felt like an impatient kid running circles around her, trying to rush her in any way possible.

Why was she moving so slowly? He knew she just woke up, but babies were coming!

He followed her instructions as she told him how to set up for the births. They ended up putting the mothers in the same pens so they could easily access both. The goats bleated, sticking their tongues way out and stretching their necks around like they didn't know what was going on back there.

Jameson couldn't handle the fact that they were in pain

and he couldn't do anything about it. He paced back and forth, occasionally stopping to rub Josie's and Pearl's head. It's not like he knew these animals well, but they had been bunk mates for the past few nights. For some reason though, he felt pulled to them.

The storm picked up outside, the rain battering down on the metal roof making it almost too loud to hear the goats' grunts. Guardian lifted his head as if to make sure the sound still came from the storm, then he rolled over on his side with a huff. Even he acted like nothing was happening.

"It's going to be awhile. You might as well relax." Sydney sat in the far corner, leaned her head against the wall, and closed her eyes.

"Relax?" The whole thing seemed absurd. Who could relax while Josie and Pearl continued to labor and bleat?

Wind blasted outside, sending rain splattering against the walls of the barn. The storm grew in force. He looked up towards the risers, wondering if the old barn would hold. The metal roof created so much racket, he wouldn't have been able to sleep anyway.

After several more minutes of pacing, the goats lay down and panted. He walked over to each one to see if anything had changed. Then, finally, he gave in and sat across from Sydney.

"Why do goats usually birth during storms?" he asked, unable to distract himself from the anxious bubbling inside of him.

"It's called kidding."

"Kidding?"

"Yeah, and they kid during storms because it is safer."

"How is giving birth, or kidding, safer in such violent, cold, wet weather?"

"It takes the scent away on the wind. Predators can't smell them."

"Huh, well, that actually makes sense." Jameson sat back and pondered. In the animal kingdom, it was all about survival. Were they that much different though? Hadn't he stopped here for just that reason? He eyes swept to the woman across from him. Somehow he felt there was more than just survival going on here. Maybe fate, or a higher power, had more of a hand in his life than he thought.

The next few hours they rested fitfully, taking naps, and then checking on the goats. Josie started to grunt and reaching back as if to check herself. Her stomach heaved and she panted, occasionally letting out a grunting bleat.

"Syd," Jameson said as he squatted by the laboring animal. "Syd, I think something's happening."

Sydney rubbed her eyes and then moved to squat beside him. She smelled fresh and clean, and he had to stop himself from nuzzling his head into her neck to breathe the scent in deeper. The urge surprised him, and he pulled himself back to the task at hand.

When Sydney lifted Josie's tail all other thoughts stopped. A massive glob that looked like a giant bubble of mucus extended from under her tail. Jameson stood up quickly and took a step back.

"That's the kid." Sydney stood next to him, searching his eyes. "You going to be able to handle this?"

The tease in her voice egged him on. No way would he let himself show weakness. If this small slip of a woman could birth, or rather kid, goats, then he could too. "Of course," he said, doing his best to smile despite the queasiness churning in him. He was beginning to think the gal was tougher than he thought he was.

"Well, it's about to get intense now. Grab a towel and some gloves." She donned on a pair of gloves that stretched up to her elbows.

A flash of memory hit him of snapping on gloves. An image of a dead body popped up in his mind, and he leaned a hand on the railing. He saw his hand checking for a pulse on the grey body, and then he lifted wet, blond hair away from a face. He shook his head and gasped for breath.

What in the world was that?

"You okay?"

Jameson blinked a few times before focusing on multi-colored eyes belonging to Syd. The goats. The image wasn't real. Or at least it wasn't where he was right now.

"You look like you saw a ghost."

"Was close." His voice came out gruff, but she didn't step back. Instead, she put a hand on his arm.

"You want to talk about it?"

He shook his head. He would rather forget about it altogether.

Josie saved him from the memory as she struggled to get to her feet with a loud, groaning bleat.

"Here we go," Sydney said with one last look at him.

"Just tell me what to do."

"We mostly watch. They know what to do. We're only here to help if needed."

He nodded, watching the goat turn back again and lick her side. Her stomach contracted and the bubble of goo protruded a little further. With each surge, Josie grunted a little more. He couldn't help it, he took her head and petted her, whispering soothing words.

Sydney watched him. He felt her eyes burning into him, but he couldn't just let the goat struggle without some support.

"Look, Jameson," Sydney whispered. The awe in her voice caused him to give Josie's head one more scratch before he looked around her.

The bubble now had form, and beneath the membrane he could make out the tiny muzzle of a baby goat. His heart clenched. Truly birth was a miracle.

Josie gave a few more heaving pushes and the baby hung from her, the back legs still inside. It looked awkward as the kid swung side to side with Josie's efforts.

"Shouldn't we…I mean that can't be comfortable." He squeezed his hands together in effort to not reach out to give the goat a helping hand.

"It's all part of the process. Hanging like that is important." She swiped at the membrane around the kid's face. "We can take this off though. Here you go little one."

The kid gave a squeal not much different than a human baby. Again, Jameson was thrown back into a memory. He doubled over, holding tight to his knees. An infant cried as someone handed him the baby, he reached out lovingly and brought the bundle close against him. *It's alright, Uncle Jameson has you. Shh, we're going to be great pals.* The memory faded as fast as it came on, leaving him weak-kneed.

He landed forward on his knees just as the kid burst forth in a surge of liquid, falling to the straw beneath it. Sydney hastily pulled the membrane off of the goat as Josie turned and licked the wet kid. Its eyes opened and wet ears twitched. Jameson couldn't help the smile that crept across his face.

Sydney kept taking glances at him as she watched the kid get its first bath. The smile on her lips held warmth, but her eyes as they met his shone with empathy.

"You had another one," she stated.

"Yeah, a good one. I think I have a nephew, or a niece. I couldn't tell."

"That is a good one," she said before turning her attention to the kid.

Jameson followed her gaze and watched as the tiny goat struggled to move and use its legs. It mewed, a sound that tugged on Jameson's heart, allowing flashes of a baby in his arms.

"I think the memories are triggered by sound." He rubbed his face. So much was happening right now. He should be focused on the kidding, not his past, but excitement filtered through him with the flashes of memory.

"That's good to know, right? Maybe we need to subject you to a whole bunch of different sounds and get those memories flowing."

"Might not be a bad idea." He smiled at the woman who seemed to understand exactly what he needed.

Pearl let out a painful bleat as she rocked to her knees. A tale-tell blob extended from her now.

"Right now though, I think we have our hands full." Jameson watched Sydney as she took two quick steps to the other mama goat. She moved with confidence and poise, her eyes lit with excitement. Even with the memories flowing in, he found himself enjoying this experience, feeling as if he belonged here in this moment with her.

## ~7~

Sydney rested back against the splintered wood of the barn wall, waves of exhaustion and elation rushing through her. The storm had eased. Only a light pattering of rain bounced off the metal roof. A rooster crowed from near the coop. To the bird, a sunrise was a sunrise whether he could see the sun or not.

Jameson settled himself beside her. She reached over and patted his leg. The touch shot tingles through her, igniting what energy she had left.

"You did great." Pulling her hand off his leg felt like disengaging two powerful magnets.

"Thank you," he said, his voice sounding more excited than tired. "That was quite the experience!"

"Yeah," she said, watching the four kids guzzle milk from their mamas. "Little miracles."

"I wasn't sure little Brownie over there was going to make it."

"Brownie, huh?" she asked, peeking over at him.

"Well, yeah, she looks like a chocolate brownie." He shrugged, a content smile making his eyes wrinkle.

A warm tingling started in her chest and spread throughout her. She tried to stop it, but the feeling wasn't under her control. It felt too good having him here with her, kidding the goats and enjoying the aftermath together. They had made a great team too.

She shook her head and closed her eyes. *Don't go there, Sydney.* It would hurt too much when he left. Yet what if he stayed? The idea danced around inside of her, making her pulse quicken. She let the dream play for a bit, but then sobered.

"Do you think you're married?" she blurted out, heat rising to her cheeks.

"No," he answered immediately.

She sat up and looked at him. His green eyes still held the glow from experiencing the births. His lips tilted up to the right in a satisfied smile.

"How would you know?" she asked.

"So far, those spontaneous, immediate answers seem to be accurate." His eyes took on an intense stare. "Besides, it just doesn't seem right. Those memory flashes are coming more frequently. Certain things set them off, like emotions, or sounds, like the snapping of the gloves or the kid mewing. They set off fleeting flashes of remembrances."

"I'm happy for you, Jameson."

"Like that. My name has familiar tug to it." He held up his left hand, a massive palm and thick fingers. "Besides, no evidence of a ring."

"Some men don't wear them," she countered.

"Well, I didn't have any tugs when you mentioned it. It just doesn't seem to fit."

Sydney sat back against the wall, a slow smile spreading. "Maybe you're not into women."

A chuckle rolled from out of Jameson before he sat up and turned towards her. "I assure you that is not the case."

Her heart quickened and try as she might, she couldn't take her eyes away from his encompassing gaze. "How can you be sure?"

His tongue darted out to wet his lips, and he leaned forward, just slightly, but enough she could feel the heat radiating off his body. "I wouldn't have the urge to do this."

That warm tingling turned into an all-out fire. Yearning spread throughout her. Her heart raced, tummy clenched, and she couldn't convince her body to stop moving forward towards those now moist, kissable lips. His warm breath smelled of coffee and desire.

She hadn't kissed a man, nor even wanted to, for two years. That physical need took control, never once even allowing rational thought a chance. They leaned closer and closer, until only a half inch apart. Their lips brushed together and electricity zipped into her belly—

*Honk, honk!*

They jerked back, their eyes searching each other. Her heart paused before kicking into overdrive. Who could be here? She needed to go out and check, but she couldn't move away from Jameson. The magnetic pull wouldn't release her.

A truck door slammed in the driveway. "Sydney!"

Her eyes went wide, and the spell between Jameson and her broke so suddenly she flung back against the wall. She stood up in such a rush the world went black for a moment. Jameson's hand reached out and steadied her.

"You alright?" he asked, his deep voice somehow an octave lower. Amusement gleamed in his eyes. He wouldn't be amused if he knew who had just arrived or what that could mean for him.

"Wil." She shook her head. "That's Sheriff Whitmore."

"Sydney!" Wil's voice sing-songed.

Jameson's eyes narrowed before glancing along the barn's wall. He found a knothole to peer out into the driveway.

"I'll get him out of here." She slapped the hay off of her clothes, breathed in deep, and took a step away.

"Syd." Jameson's large hand grasped hers. Something shot through his eyes, an emotion she hadn't yet seen in him. One she couldn't quite place. Was it fear, anger, or something else?

"It's alright, Jameson. Just stay out of sight." She squared her shoulders and walked from the barn. She could feel Jameson's eyes on her. Somehow knowing he watched her lent comfort as she walked towards the man her childhood crush had grown up to become.

"Sydney!" Wil sang again, almost to the house now.

"Here, Wil," she called out, allowing her exhaustion to show through.

"Oh, there you are." He turned towards her with a wide grin under a thin mustache. He tipped the beige Sheriff's hat up, allowing his sandy hair to peek out.

"Why are you here, Wil?" She stopped as he reached her, letting the rain mist down and plaster the hair onto her head. She wished she had her hat.

"Always to the point. Just one of the many things I love about you." He smiled his come-and-get-me smile that used to melt her heart. These days, though, it made her sick.

"So?" She shoved her fists onto her hips, allowing her annoyance at him ruining her first kiss with Jameson to show through. Her heart hammered…she had kissed Jameson. Well, their lips had touched at least. Wait, maybe she should be thanking Wil for breaking that moment. What in the world had she been thinking?

"Can't an old friend come a'visiting?"

Sydney narrowed her eyes, trying to focus on him and not the tingling that still burned her lips.

"Okay, okay. Dang girl, when did you become so serious?" He chuckled hoarsely, a sound that caused her to cringe.

When she had spent her summers here, a carefree-Sydney came out, but back home she had always been serious. Guess though he had never really seen that serious side of her. Did that free-spirit-of-a-girl still exist somewhere in her?

"There's been reports of criminal activity in and around the county."

Fear gripped her heart along with all her thoughts, but she pushed through.

"Did the Phillips boy tip over the Anderson's cows again? Or maybe someone is stealing chickens? Should I lock up my hen house at night?" She did her best to fill her voice with sarcasm, but the world felt as if it closed in on her.

"Oh Sydney, you always have so many questions. Your foolhardy stubbornness of being out here all alone is going to get you in trouble one of these days." His words trailed off as he met her narrowed eyes.

"We live in a small, safe community, Wil. What do I have to be worried about?"

"Looks can be deceiving." He leaned towards her and lowered his voice. "There's been gang activity in the area."

She tried to hold her laughter in, but it burst forth.

His look of importance deflated, rapidly replaced by the false cockiness he had acquired over the years.

"You mean Butch Cassidy is back with his gang?"

"This isn't a joke, Sydney." He hooked his thumbs in his belt buckles, for once his tone subdued.

Her laughter died instantly as her mind whirled with what this all meant. "What kind of gang would be interested in our small town?"

"Drug trafficking, what else?" He shrugged and took a step towards her.

Sydney's mouth hung open and fear filled her veins. Not again... She looked back to the barn before she caught herself. James couldn't be involved in a drug gang, could he?

"And you're out here, all alone." His finger reached out to brush her cheek.

A decade ago that touch would have had her high for a week. Today it caused a shudder of contempt to crawl through her and mix with the trepidation building up. He was a married man, though he hadn't been forthcoming with that information.

Her mind traveled to two years ago. She had only been back on the ranch for two months when he came for his first visit. Learning how to run this place without her aunt and uncle took time. Wil had arrived right when she needed help. She had been struggling with a few goats who had gotten loose while Homer had run into town to get parts to fix the fence.

Wil easily helped her round up and pen the stray goats, coming to her rescue just as he used when they were kids. He had stayed for lunch, and she couldn't help but notice he wore no ring. She wasn't quite ready to jump into a relationship after what she had just fled, but she enjoyed the attention and couldn't stop the hope that crept in her with what became weekly visits.

It wasn't until the town gossip who ran the local grocer watched their interaction and clucked her tongue. After Wil left, Sydney had taken her items up to check out.

"Now Miss Campbell," the grocer's shrill voice had admonished her. "You shouldn't go flirting with married men like that."

Heat had burned her cheeks only to drop into the fire that grew in her belly with those words. "Wil is married?" she had asked, barely able to hear her voice over the pounding of her heart.

"Yes, and to a sweet girl, mind you. It's been almost five years now."

That day she had decided she was finished with men. They were all liars, thieves, and abusers...all but her dear Uncle Joe.

She took a step back from Wil as her memories flashed through, igniting that fire in her belly which reminded her of her hardened heart. "I'm not alone."

Wil's eyes tilted in mirth. "Sure, Sydney, but animals don't count." His chuckle turned into a wheezing cough. He should have put that first cigarette down when she had told him to all those years ago.

"I have Homer."

His eyes scanned the drive where Homer usually parked his quad. "He isn't here now."

"He will be shortly."

A thump sounded from the barn, and she turned in time to see Jameson's shadow leave the knothole. Wil's eyes shot towards her and then focused intently towards the sound. He took a step towards the barn.

"If Homer ain't here, then who's banging around in that barn?"

Sydney caught his shoulder, plastering on a smile, hoping that he couldn't hear her pounding heart. "Just the new kids. They were just born this morning." She stifled a yawn, something she didn't have to fake. "I'm exhausted."

He hadn't moved, his stare burning a hole in the barn.

She slid her hand from his shoulder and down his arm. She quelled the uneasy feeling in her stomach as her fingers wrapped around his hand, a hand that seemed small after Jameson's. Wil turned his gaze towards her, an eyebrow raised.

"Why don't you come out of the rain and have a cup of coffee with me? I need to sit down." The smile covering her lips felt strained. She looked away to try to hide that fact from Wil.

"That is mighty tempting, Sydney." He twirled a finger in the palm of her hand, and she took a deep breath in to stop the bile rising up. "The boys need me at the office, so I'll have to take a rain check." A raspy laugh wheezed from between his lips. "Get it, rain check?"

"Yeah, I get it." She never knew smiling could be so painful. She pulled her hand from out of his slimy grasp, trying to stop the reaction of wiping it off on her dirty jeans.

"If you see anything suspicious, you call me." He took her chin in his thumb and finger. "Night or day. You got my cell."

"Of course," she said, keeping her voice light and using every bit of her willpower to not tear her face from his grasp.

His thumb swept across her lips as he took his hand away. "I'll be back to take you up on that coffee." He winked as he climbed into his Sheriff's truck.

As soon as his truck turned back down the driveway, she wiped her mouth on the sleeve of her jacket and swiped a hand down her now soaked jeans. *What a jerk!* She narrowed her eyes as the rain covered his tracks, her body shaking in anger.

"So, that's your Sheriff?" Jameson's voice startled her.

She pulled her eyes off the drive and connected with the brilliant green of his. Drugs and gang activity in the area...could that gang be responsible for leaving Jameson on the side of the road? Fear pounded in her chest, a familiar trembling that she didn't like.

"Yeah."

"What's the situation between you two?" That furrow between his brows returned. Was that jealousy lining his voice?

"Nothing." She wiped at the rain dripping into her eyes. "There's nothing between us. He's married." She turned and headed towards the house. She needed to sit down before she fell into the mud puddles beneath her boots.

"He doesn't act married," Jameson added as he followed her.

"Exactly. I told you. I don't trust him." She slipped off her boots and hung her dripping jacket from one of the wooden pegs next to the door.

Jameson mimicked her movements, and then opened the door for her to step through. She froze once inside the house, completely drained. A large, warm hand rested on her shoulder.

"You're shaking, Syd."

She nodded, unsure if it was from cold, exhaustion, emotional turmoil, fear, or a bit of it all.

"Go take a hot shower and then rest. I'll take care of the morning chores."

She turned towards him, knowing full well he would read the fear in her eyes, but needing to know. "You heard what Wil said?"

"Yeah," he said, letting the word drop as if its heaviness could no longer be held. He put both hands on her shoulders. "We can deal with that after you rest."

The heaviness of his hands filled her with an odd feeling of safety and comfort. He had a way of easing her fears and maneuvering her to follow his suggestions. As exhausted as she was, she couldn't fight it. A warning sounded in her. She would have to watch herself around him.

"About what happened back in the barn..." Her cheeks burned. She felt foolish bringing it up, but shouldn't they talk about what happened, or almost happened?

"Too soon?" His green eyes pierced her as that small crooked smile played on his lips. "I'll be more careful not let the moment carry me away next time. Now go shower and rest."

Her brain felt fuzzy and her heart fluttered. Was that what she wanted? Was it too soon? She shook her sleep-deprived head. He was right, she needed to go rest. "Thank you." Yet, as she reached the bathroom, she couldn't stop herself from turning to meet his eyes across the distance once more.

~*~

Jameson waited until he heard the shower turn on before slipping back outside. All he wanted to do at the moment was drop into the couch, but he knew if he allowed himself that luxury he wouldn't get back up. His mind roared with uneasiness. His hairs stood on end. Something was going to happen, and soon.

A rock burned within his gut. Something was going to happen, and he put an innocent, kind, amazing woman right smack dab into the middle of it. He should leave right now before the trouble following him found him here. He had no idea where he came from or who left him on the side of the road, but a little tingling inside of him told him he was involved with this gang somehow, and they would be looking for him.

He slammed his feet into the muddy boots, startling

Guardian. The dog looked at him and woofed. They stared at each other for a moment, and then Jameson donned on the slick coat and walked out into the mist. With one look back at the house, Guardian followed.

"We've got to check the perimeter, boy." Jameson found himself talking to the dog. He reached out and patted the soaked fur. It's too bad he had to leave. This place had grown on him. Guardian nuzzled into his hand, triggering another memory.

Jameson was filled with longing. He saw himself as a boy running with a golden retriever. They ran down an open field towards a river. He turned and shouted to the dog to hurry before laughing and continuing onto jump into the cool water.

"Buddy," he whispered. He remembered his childhood dog and trips to the river. He was going to get through this. He would remember who he was.

He scanned the land he had grown fond of, listened to the goats demanding their breakfast, and smiled as a deep, emotional longing filled him. Maybe after all of this had settled he would return. Would Syd want him to?

Sydney awoke to banging in the kitchen. Her heart raced, and she sat straight up in bed. Bright, mid-day sun shone through the window. She rubbed her blurry eyes and tried to tame her wild hair while memories flooded in.

Jameson must have gotten hungry. Poor guy. She fell asleep before making him breakfast.

She shook her head. She wasn't his wife, nor girlfriend, nor caretaker. In fact, she was nothing to him but a place to sleep and hide out from whatever or whomever was after him. Wil's words came back to her. Was she putting herself in danger? Wasn't that why she loved this place so much, to be far away from that kind of life?

She shoved the thoughts out as she shoved her feet into some clean jeans. She should probably start sleeping in something besides a tank top and panties with Jameson here making himself at home. Heat crept up her neck as she remembered the brief moment their lips touched. She had never had such an innocent touch leave her so charged and weak-kneed.

She couldn't let it happen again. Whatever was going on, she didn't want to be dragged into the middle of it. She didn't know if she could recover from another event like that.

Rounding the hall into the kitchen, she found Jameson standing in the middle of the room, an endearing look of bewilderment on his face. He had a loaf of homemade uncut bread, paper wrapped ham, mayo, a tomato, and lettuce all sitting on the counter.

"Hey," he said as he saw her watching him. A soft pink filled his cheeks as he looked at the items scattered throughout the kitchen.

"Forgot how to make a sandwich?" she asked, not able to hide a grin.

His face fell for an instant, and immediately she regretted the words. Mental note, *Don't joke about forgetting things with someone who has amnesia.*

"Go, sit." She pushed him lightly towards the table.

"I can do it." He squared his shoulders, not budging.

"I'm sure you can, but it's the least I can do since you just did my chores while I slept the morning away."

His ego still intact, he gave a small grin before shuffling to the table. A yawn spread through him as he stretched up, his long arms making it easy for his fingertips to brush the ceiling. His size made this house feel small. He lifted his eyebrows when he saw her watching him. A rush of heat filled her cheeks as she busied herself with making lunch.

"How were the hens? Were there many eggs?" she asked, hoping to distract them both.

"Only one."

"Well, that's pretty normal with the storm we just had."

Out of the corner of her eye, she saw his head nod, then his hand reach down to pet Mr. Paws. The cat jumped onto his lap, and Jameson relaxed back in his chair while mindlessly stroking the purring feline. He kept his eyes trained out the window until she set a plate in front of him.

"Thank you," he said, meeting her gaze. Sorrow and loss lived in his eyes. What had he been thinking about?

"You're welcome. Thank you for helping out. I can't believe how long I slept."

He gifted her another grin before taking a bite. Once he had cleared his mouth enough to speak, he said, "It's the least I can do. It has been kind of you to allow me to stay here."

The way he said it made her feel like he was saying goodbye. Her heart froze, along with her hand holding the sandwich. The bite she had just taken stuck in her throat. No matter how many times she attempted, the food couldn't get past the lump that had immediately formed there.

"It would be advisable for me to move on." He set his lunch down and looked back out the window.

After several swallows of water, her food finally found its way to her stomach, where it sat heavy, almost as heavy as the doom that filled the air. How could she both fear him leaving and staying? She didn't know, but that fear sent her skin in a wash of prickly goosebumps.

"Where would you go?" She barely whispered the words, afraid that they would set into motion the turmoil that seemed to be hovering over them.

He shrugged. "Whatever part I play in all this, I don't want to put you into harm's way."

The intensity in his eyes held her captive. She wanted to beg him to stay. She wanted to tell him that she could handle anything thrown at her. Yet fear-laden memories engulfed her. Before she could stop, she relived the terrifying day.

She had finished dinner she had made for her then-boyfriend and was on her way to the bathroom when men in black, armored suits and masks broke into her house, shoved guns in her face and yelled at her to get down, put her hands on her head.

She had no idea they were the good guys until they had her ex-boyfriend in cuffs and sat her on the couch. They had barraged her with question after question of things that she had been clueless of. The whole time they interrogated her, she watched them tear through her house, ripping cushions, breaking vases, and tearing up the carpet.

The DEA agents were just as shocked that she had no clue about her ex-boyfriend's activities as she was that he had been doing anything illegal. The event left her a nervous wreck. For many months afterward, she had jumped at every sound, fear lancing and her heart beating in panic.

It had only been a week after that event when she got the call about Uncle Joe and Aunt Meg. She left her ripped up, broken house and moved up here for a much needed change.

"Hey." Jameson's large, warm hand swallowed hers as he broke her reverie. "You okay?"

"Yeah," she said, trying to shake off the memory. His hand on hers eased the fear that had built up. Her shoulders relaxed and she found herself breathing easier. When he touched her like this she wanted to plead with him to stay. She wouldn't fear as long as he was near.

Jameson pulled his hand off hers and an emptiness filled it. He stood, and his eyes swept across the house before finally resting back on her. "I…If you don't mind, I would rather wait until first light to, uh, to leave."

"Of course," she said and looked away quickly. Her eyes brimmed, and there was no way she would let him see the tears that were about to spill.

He nodded and walked out the screen door, his sandwich left half-eaten on his plate.

~*~

Jameson swung the hammer with all of his pent up emotion behind it. The nail had practically disappeared in the fence post. He straightened, wiped the sweat off his brow, rolled his injured shoulder and shook out his stiff leg. He had to do this. He had to leave. She wasn't safe with him here.

He needed her safe.

Sydney had welcomed him in with no memory, with no real reason, and gave him a place to stay, home cooked meals and a life…a life, he realized more every minute he stayed, he wanted. A simple, no drama, small-town life.

~*~

All the rest of the day, Sydney's mind warred with itself. Jameson had appeared at her doorstep, coincidentally right after she wished for a man just like him. Could Aunt Mag be right? Could his presence, and the timing of it, be more than a coincidence?

She kneaded the goat milk soap mixture together, enjoying the feeling on her skin. It felt good to do something with her hands, though if it had required more brain power maybe her mind wouldn't be waging war against itself. Wiping off the creamy goop, she grabbed the molds and began pouring the soap in. Aunt Mag and Uncle Joe never made soap. This was her contribution to the ranch, something that was all hers.

Jameson and she worked so well together. Her mind started going again. Yeah, but who knew who he really was? He might get his memory back and flee this ranch life and her as abruptly as he entered it. Jameson's large hands were capable of heavy-duty work and may have been made through hard labor, but their smoothness showed he hadn't used them for hard ranch work for years.

Guardian padded along beside her as she walked to the house to start dinner. A pounding from the chicken coup told her that Jameson was fixing the base which he said was wobbly. Well, if tonight was to be his last night here, she would make a meal to remember. She pulled out two steaks from the fridge, a couple potatoes from the basement, and put the bread that she had set out to rise earlier into the oven.

She flipped the steaks on the barbeque, enjoying the sizzling aroma. Pink spread across the sky in a gorgeous display of a Wyoming sunset. A peace filled her as it always did when she appreciated this ranch and the beautiful countryside it sat in.

Jameson's tall silhouette against the perfect backdrop walked towards her. He tugged on his cowboy hat, and the breath caught in her throat.

How could she let him leave?

The night gave the perfect atmosphere so she set up dinner on the porch. They ate mostly in silence, Guardian at their feet.

"Guess you'll have to find another replacement before August..." Jameson's mouth tugged up ever so slightly.

"Too bad, I thought I had found the perfect match." Once the words left her mouth she realized how not only flirtatious they sounded, but how true they were.

Jameson and she worked well together. He finished projects he started, he had an eye for what needed to be fixed, and they had a way of intuitively knowing what the other needed without words being spoken. The kidding had made that obvious. Even Homer and she didn't work that well together, and he had guided her since she was a child.

What would it have been like if she and Jameson had met under different circumstances?

When she finally met Jameson's eyes, she realized he waged his own battle. "Maybe, if I get this all settled before summer's over, I could come back."

Sydney's heart sped up with the thought. "I would like that."

He probably had said that just to help ease the transition of him leaving, but maybe, just maybe, his words held some truth.

"Have you thought more about going to the authorities?" she asked, hoping to distract him from her last statement. "I mean, you have to be on the good side right?"

"The *good* side." His one sided grin gripped her heart. "You're probably right. Doing drugs doesn't seem to fit."

"Well, you talk like a cop...or something along those lines."

"Yeah...I have noticed that tendency."

"So, why not go to the authorities? I bet they could figure out who you are."

"I don't know." He rubbed his hand over his short hair and scratched his cheek. His beard had grown in over the last few days. It didn't look bad on him, but she didn't think he was comfortable with it either. "Something just feels…off, like I shouldn't go there."

"Do you really believe there are drug gangs working around this area?"

"Yes." He nodded as he said it. "Drug trafficking happens everywhere."

Sydney jumped when the phone rang from inside the house. Who would be calling? She widened her eyes and looked to Jameson.

"That's the first time I have heard your phone ring," he said, his brow knitting.

"I don't get many calls." She walked into the house with Jameson following close on her heels, an uneasiness settling into her stomach. "Hello?" she answered.

"Miss Syd." Homer's voice filled with urgency.

"Homer? Are you alright?" Her eyes met Jameson's and familiar jabs of fear poked her chest. Jameson bent his head down so he could hear the phone as well. It seemed natural, and she turned the phone out so he could hear easier.

"Yes, yes, Miss Syd. I was just coming back from town and thought you should know a strange black SUV is sitting in your driveway. It just seemed off. Do you want me to call Wil?"

Jameson and Sydney caught each other's eyes. He shook his head and a look of warning filled him.

"Did you happen to catch the license plate, Homer?" Jameson spoke into the receiver.

"Jameson, what are you doing on Miss Syd's phone?" Homer's attempt to cover a chuckle didn't work.

"We were eating dinner, Homer," she said quickly to stop his thoughts. "Did you see the license plate or anything else?"

"Sure, sure. Well, let me try to remember…they were Wyoming plates…something either XY14 or YX41. I can't remember the other numbers. The windows were tinted. Just sat strange with me. I hope I'm not worrying you,

Syd."

"You did the right thing, Homer." Jameson had a professional quality to his voice that Sydney had occasionally noticed before. "If you remember anything else or something suspicious, please contact us right away."

"Of course. You sure you don't want me to call Wil? He would send a deputy out there to shoo them away at least."

One look at Jameson, and she knew what he wanted. "We'll take care of it, Homer. Thank you so much for letting me know."

"Okay," he said, hesitantly. "Give me a call if you need me. Otherwise I'll see you in the morning."

"Thank you, again, Homer. Sleep well," she said, trying to sound reassuring though her heart pounded a million miles a minute.

"Goodnight, Syd."

"Goodnight." She hung up the phone and slowly raised her eyes to meet Jameson's. His face had taken on a serious, yet expressionless appearance—eyes focused, yet no emotion crossed his features. *What have I gotten myself into…again?*

"It's going to be alright, Syd, but…" He rubbed a hand across his short hair, and for a split second his eyes took on a look of uncertainty. "If it won't, if you're okay, it would be safer if I stayed in the house tonight."

Was it wrong that the first feeling that rushed through her was relief? Shouldn't she be embarrassed or fearful of this stranger sleeping in her little house? Yet, a warmth of safety flooded her. Jameson wouldn't let anything happen to her. She knew it. She didn't know how, but she knew he would and could protect her from whatever would come.

"I'm not trying to be forward." Jameson shifted his weight and looked down at his feet.

She realized then she had been debating her sanity for who-knows-how-long while he watched her uncertainly.

"No, I know. Yes, that would make me feel safer." She scanned the small living room, the recliner, and small love seat. Not really a place to sleep there. The office held the small twin bed that she had slept in as a girl. She almost laughed aloud trying to picture his imposing size fitting into that small trundle bed.

Jameson cocked his head to the side as his eyebrows furrowed. "What's so funny?"

"I, uh, the spare bed is quite small." She shrugged.

"I won't be sleeping much anyway." He nodded to the living room. "That recliner will do just fine."

"If you say so," she said. A flutter began in her stomach as she thought of the large queen bed, but she shook her head. *No way, girl, you are not going there!*

"Guardian will bark if…if a car or someone comes around?" Jameson asked.

"He did when you arrived, didn't he?"

A one-sided grin cracked his serious expression, and her heart pitter-pattered. "Yes, yes, he did."

She nodded before stepping away from temptation and went outside to clear the table on the patio. She couldn't help but peer down the long drive that faded off into darkness. What was that SUV doing there? Would they come here tonight?

When she brought the dishes back into the house, she watched as Jameson systematically checked each window, locked it, pulled the curtains closed, and moved on to the next. His assured movements seemed routine and habitual. She realized she still stood frozen as her arms grew heavy. Her cheeks burned as she finally took the dishes to the sink and began washing them.

With the dishes drying in the rack, she put the last two slices of birthday cake on plates. She found Jameson on the dark porch, sitting with his back against the house and his eyes constantly scanning the tree-lined property.

"Anything?" she asked, doing her best to keep the tremor from her voice.

"No," he replied in a quiet voice.

She handed him a plate of cake and sat on the chair next to him. The night looked and sounded like any other night: crickets chirped, the frogs from the watering pond sung, horses snorted, goats occasionally bleated, and Guardian gave the occasional grunt in his sleep. Sydney allowed the peace to flow through her, easing the pounding of her heart and washing out the memories trying to invade her mind.

"Do you often bake cakes?" he asked, a hint of humor in his voice.

"No." She laughed, not meeting his eyes.

"Happy late birthday," he whispered.

The bite she had just swallowed stuck in her throat. She coughed and pounded her chest. "What?" she asked, once she could talk again. She met his eyes and even in the darkness she could see their intensity. Her heart pounded again as she realized he knew. "How?"

"The candle holes and little drips of wax." He shrugged. "Syd, why are you alone?"

The seriousness of his question left a fluttering in her chest as nervousness filled her. She lowered the plate to her lap, trying to keep the fork from tinkling against it in her shaking hands.

"Maybe I just like being alone." She jutted her chin out, trying to pretend she did. Well, a part of her did. The other side though really enjoyed the company of the man beside her, and it yearned to never be alone again.

Jameson raised his eyebrows. Yeah, he knew her too well, and in only a few days. "You try to hide it, but you're scared, and not just what a normal person would feel. You have experience with feeling this way."

Her eyes scrunched together and her throat tightened. Why did he have to go and read into her like that? She stood up abruptly and took the empty plate from his lap. The screen door didn't slam so she knew he had entered behind her, but she couldn't turn away from the sink. She washed the plates to procrastinate, yet his eyes bored into her the entire time. He wasn't going to let this go.

He stood between the kitchen and dining area, arms across his chest and eyes brilliantly green. Her hands shook, so she kept them busy and made a pot of coffee. When she no longer had any excuse to be in the kitchen, she finally met his intense gaze.

"If something goes down, it would be helpful if I knew what had happened so I could gauge how you will react." He kept his voice steady and professional.

Sydney stood there, locked in his gaze, her throat tight and fear coursing through her veins until the coffee pot stopped gurgling. With a nod, she filled two mugs and motioned to the living room. Handing Jameson his cup, she plopped into the worn loveseat. A flash of Aunt Mag crocheting while Uncle Joe read aloud filled her mind briefly—the simple days.

Jameson sat carefully in the recliner, never taking his eyes off her.

"I've had progressively bad choices in men," she started with a resigned sigh. She had never talked to anyone about this, not even her best friend, who in truth she hadn't talked to in months, okay more than a year. "My first serious boyfriend cheated on me. The second, his verbal abuse finally turned physical before I broke it off. And the last...the last one had me fooled the entire time. That is until the DEA stormed into my house and held me under gunpoint while they tore through all my belongings. I was an emotional wreck, and still get shaky when I think about it."

There, she said it. She actually breathed a little easier, having it out in the open. Summarized like that, it didn't sound all too bad. So, she had bad taste in men. What did that say for Jameson then? She watched him out of the corner of her eye, unable to meet the power of his intense gaze.

Jameson's expression hardened. The fingers holding his

coffee mug turned white. His jawed clenched. It was the first time she really saw him angry. Then his eyes unfocused, and he sat back for what felt like an hour, but was probably only a few minutes. When he looked at her again, something had shifted.

"What?" she asked, knowing something internal had occurred.

"I had a flash of a memory." He ran a hand over his short hair. "I can't quite hold it, but it's there."

"They'll come back," she said, a small smile softening her face.

"I'm sorry you went through all of that, Syd," he said with a hint of anger in his voice.

She nodded and eased back into the sofa.

"You deserve better than those men," he said through clenched teeth.

She allowed a small chuckle to bubble out and then set her cup on the coffee table. She pulled her legs up under her and rested her head on the back of the couch. "Why do you think I'm here?" Mr. Paws jumped up into her lap, and she happily stroked him. "Here, I don't have to worry about the constant questions or well-meaning friends trying to set me up. It's just me and the animals. I'm good with them." She yawned, a weariness filling her.

Jameson's eyebrows furrowed, and he leaned forward, elbows on his knees.

The coffee had done no good. Her eyes felt heavy. It took too much effort to keep them open any longer. Her eyes closed of their own accord. She felt the exhaustion consuming her, numbing her to the world.

"You don't have to be alone to be treated right, Syd."

"Oh, I know. That was my birthday wish," she murmured and snuggled further into the couch.

"Birthday wish?" He breathed out the question.

"Mmhmm." She scarcely uttered the sound.

She was barely aware of Jameson rising and then felt the last blanket Aunt Mag crocheted cover her. He gently tucked a stray hair behind her ear and pulled the blanket around her shoulders.

"I'll keep you safe, Syd. I will protect you."

His words filled her with warmth as the world faded, and she was lost to dreams of what life could be in a simpler time.

~*~

Jameson paced the house as quietly as possible, which was difficult to do as anger surged through him. He wanted to find those stupid men who had mistreated Syd and show them what fear tasted like. How could anyone even think of treating the angel Syd was with anything less than respect and the love she deserved?

A low growl emitted from his throat. Outside Guardian shifted, causing the screen to strike against the door with a thud that sent Jameson's heart racing. He checked out the window, but no movement could be seen. The dog hadn't heard anything either, otherwise he wouldn't still be dreaming.

Syd moaned softly in her sleep. He walked towards her, resisting the urge to brush back the hair that had fallen over her sweet face. If she were his, she would never feel fear again. He would make sure of it.

How could he leave her now? The men looking for him knew, or at least thought, he might be here. If he left, she would be alone, unprotected, and an easy target.

A few goats bleated and Jameson peered out the window towards the pens. The bright moon lent good light to see an expanse of the ranch. A couple goats moved around before lying down once more.

Jameson rubbed a hand down his face and blinked his dry eyes. He needed sleep. Lowering himself into the recliner, he let his eyes rest on Sydney's sleeping form. Every movement she made caused tremors to course through him as he tried to memorize her beautiful face and angelic presence.

He would protect her at whatever cost, and if he made

it out of this, he would come back. If she allowed him, he would show her how a man should treat a woman.

# ~9~

The rooster crowing broke into the comfort of Sydney's sleep. Slowly she became aware of her stiff body and a crimp in her neck. She tried to stretch out only to find her body trapped in the confines of the love seat. Her eyes shot open to green eyes watching her. An amused smile turned up Jameson's full lips. Her heart hammered as she did her best to rub the sleep from her. How long had he been watching?

"Good morning," he said, his deep voice soothing.

"Morning," she mumbled, before narrowing her eyes. "How long have you been awake?"

"Pretty much all night." He shrugged. "Not a sound from Guardian, or otherwise."

"Well, that's good." She sat up and stretched. "That couch is not comfortable."

"You looked so peaceful, I couldn't bring myself to wake you."

She rubbed the kink in her neck and yawned again. "You should get some rest." She peeked out the window. The sun hadn't risen over the mountains yet, but its light lightened the sky. Guardian must have heard her voice for he woofed his morning greeting and demand.

"Chores need to be done, and I should check the perimeter before you go out, especially alone."

"I have a gun," she said with a shrug.

A rumble sounded down the drive. She cocked her head to listen and Jameson rose, joining her at the window. Homer rode his quad to his normal parking spot. Jameson let out a breath. It tickled her neck, and her body suddenly flushed with heat. An urge to feel his lips on hers again coursed through her. She closed her eyes and stepped away from him before she did something that would later cause her pain.

"See, I won't be alone." She walked down the hall towards the restroom. "Go rest. Take my bed. It will fit you better."

"Your bed?" He shuffled his feet and a soft pink filled in behind his growing beard.

"Yeah, I won't be needing it." She stopped at the bathroom door. "Go on. You need to sleep."

When she exited the bathroom ten minutes later, she realized she needed to grab some clean clothes. She tip-toed back to the bedroom. The door stood open. Peeking in she saw Jameson sprawled out in her bed, breathing deeply. The breath caught in her throat. He looked good in her bed. His bare chest peeked above the covers. His shirt and pants sat neatly stacked on the nightstand. Her heart raced thinking of him in her bed almost naked.

He shifted in his sleep, and she chastised herself for staring at him. She backed out the doorway, deciding it wouldn't hurt her to wear the same clothes until she took a shower that evening. She quietly walked back down the hall and began her morning routine.

\*\*\*

A few hours later, Sydney carried the last pail of goat milk into the cheese room. Guardian barked from beside her, making her jump and almost tip over the full bucket. Her breath froze, and her heart went into overdrive. The bucket sloshed, goat milk spilling over as she hastily dropped it. She ran to the barn, grabbed her gun, and ran to the door to sneak a look. Was it the dark SUV? A truck door slammed before she made it to the door. Then she heard the tell-tale sing-song of her name.

Wil.

"Sydney!" he called again.

Her fists clenched. He was making this into an unwelcome habit. She swiped her hair behind her ears, took a deep breath, and then strutted out to the annoying visitor.

"Back already?" she asked, noticing she didn't quite conceal her annoyance.

"Well, couldn't pass up the invitation to coffee." He winked as he greeted her with a kiss on the cheek.

A kiss? Really? What had gotten into him? "Coffee?"

"I know. I know. It's late morning already. Something came up at the office that delayed me."

Her eyes narrowed and fists shoved into her sides.

"Brunch?" He raised his eyebrows a couple times. "I'm feeling hungry." He licked his lips in a way that made her skin crawl.

"You want me to cook for you?" She heard the hostility in her voice, not that it seemed to make it to Wil.

"Since you asked, sure!" he said, grabbing her hand and pulling her towards the house.

It took her a few steps until the shock wore off. Who did he think he was? "What are you doing?"

He turned towards her with his wide smile. "Why having some brunch with a pretty lady."

Her heels dug in, and she yanked her hand from his. "Wil, you're a married man."

He shrugged, his smile never fading. "What does that have to do with anything?" He kept walking towards the house.

Anger consumed her in liquid lava. It stopped her brain from working. It wasn't until he opened the screen door that reality hit her. Jameson was in the house! Her heart raced as she ran towards him.

"Wil, stop!" She purposely raised her voice, hoping Jameson was a light sleeper.

He froze in the doorway, a curious look on his face. "Geez, Sydney, it's just a meal between old friends."

She reached him on the porch, standing in the doorway, and frantically searched for a way to keep him out of the house. "I…I don't want people talking," she stuttered lamely.

His hand reached out and traced her jaw. "No one will ever know, baby."

"What? No!" She stepped back. "That's not what I meant. I'm a moral woman. You are married."

"I know how you crushed on me." He hooked his thumbs in his belt loop, a cheeky smile on his face.

"That was a decade ago, Wil."

"So, it was." He shrugged and stepped into the house.

"No, I...I..." She blew out an exasperated breath and tried to control her racing mind. "Wil, I need you to leave."

"Why, baby? You have nothing to hide from me." He took her hand and pulled her into the house with him. "No one will know." He yanked her against him in what she thought he believed was a seductive move.

"No, Wil." She put both hands up against his chest and pushed. He didn't budge. "Please, don't do this. You need to leave."

"Come on, baby. I know you've wanted this since you came back. Don't you think we waited long enough?" He leaned in until his mustache tickled her lip.

She pushed his chest, turned her head, and finally instinct took over. Her body went limp, and she slipped from his grasp. As she hit the floor, she saw him fly backwards. She looked up and saw Wil on the ground with a seething Jameson in hastily pulled on, but still unbuttoned pants, standing over him, his fists clenched at his sides.

"I believe the lady asked you to leave...twice." Jameson's voice came out from gritted teeth, deeper and darker than she had ever heard it.

"What?! Who are you?" Wil shouted as he scrambled back up. He looked down Jameson's naked chest and unbuttoned pants and then to Sydney. His hand instinctively hovered over his holstered gun.

"Wil, I tried to tell you." She ran over to stand between

him and Jameson. The last thing she needed was that kind of drama. She snuck a glance at Jameson, his eyes seemed to shoot out fury, and they never left Wil. "This is, he's…"

"Her fiancé," Jameson's voice shot out.

A tingle zapped down Sydney's body, filling her with fire. Why did that sound so good?

Wil looked from her to Jameson and back to her. "Well, dang girl, why didn't you say something?" Then he peered closer at Jameson, a perplexing look washing over his face. "Wait, you haven't left town for almost two years…and you haven't had visitors."

"How would you know that?" Jameson growled.

"It's a small town." He shrugged, a cocky expression covering his face like he just figured out a secret.

"We met online," she said hastily.

"Online?" Wil tugged on his hat, uncertainty playing in his eyes.

"Yeah, you know, a dating site." She shrugged and stepped closer to Jameson.

"And you're engaged?" He looked down at her hand. "I see no ring."

"Well, what can I say?" Jameson's voice had calmed, though she could still hear the edge. He pulled her into him and kissed the top of her head. Heat filled her, settling in the pit of her stomach. It felt so good in his arms, charade or not. "It was spontaneous. One look and I knew I couldn't let her get away."

Sydney looked up at those green eyes that smiled down at her. Why did it feel like he was being honest with that statement? For a moment she forgot the situation they were in, and she let the feeling of those words, of being in Jameson's arms, of safety, fill her.

"Well, then, Mr.?" Wil asked and reality flooded back into her.

"Ja—" Jameson started.

"Jake Monroe," Sydney interrupted quickly, though she wasn't sure why. "Meet Sheriff Wil Whitmore."

"Well, Mr. Monroe, I guess I misunderstood the invitation." Wil brushed off his clothes and threw his shoulders back.

"I would say so, *Sheriff*." Jameson's voice tightened again, and the slur to Wil's title didn't pass him up.

"I'll take my leave then, but watch your backs."

"What's that supposed to mean, Wil?" She faced him, her hands on her hips.

"That means, there's been more sightings of that gang I told you about. Word is, they're looking for someone." He stared pointedly at Jameson. "I don't want to see Sydney get hurt."

"She won't as long as I'm around." Jameson put his arm around her again and pulled her out of the way so Wil could leave.

"I see that." He turned towards her. "Sydney, if you need anything, you know how to get a hold of me." He tipped his hat and strode out the door to his truck.

Jameson and Sydney watched from the screen door as his dust settled in the driveway. Neither of them had moved. His arm still hugged her close to him. She savored the feeling of safety and the feeling of being in this together.

His eyes met hers. The pull felt magnetic and powerful. She wanted to stand up on tippy-toes and press her lips against his, but she couldn't, could she? Should she? Her heart raced and the world faded—all except Jameson, his eyes, his lips, his touch, his smell, his protective presence.

"Meow." Mr. Paws weaved in and out of their legs, breaking the moment.

"Online dating, huh?" Jameson's eyes were bright with amusement.

"Fiancé?" she countered.

He shrugged, reluctantly letting her go.

"Not boyfriend, cousin, brother?"

"It's the first thing that came to mind." He rubbed his head again. "Thanks for the save. Almost gave him the only piece of information I know about myself."

"Yeah, don't know how that came from me so quickly."

"Used to making things up?" he asked, eyebrows raised.

"We all have our fantasies, I guess." She laughed, trying to ease the emotions that the last twenty minutes had overwhelmed her with.

"Where's Homer by the way?"

"Ran into town for some grain."

"You should have woke me." His jaw clenched again.

She eyed him curiously. "I didn't expect Wil to show up, nor him to make a move like that. He never has before. Lately he has seemed different, cockier." Her body went rigid. She didn't have to defend herself. Jameson wasn't really her fiancé, and she didn't have to answer to him.

"Right now, Syd," Jameson's voice softened, easing the bristling in her, "you have to expect the unexpected." He rubbed a hand over his head with more force than before. "I am sorry I brought you into this mess. It wasn't my intention. I should have never stayed."

"Not like you had much choice," she shot back at him.

"I can't leave now." He locked eyes with her, that intensity back and burning bright. "We'll have to ride this one out to the finish, together. I promise, though, I will keep you safe."

~*~

While Sydney finished taking care of the chores, Jameson snuck around the property as stealthily as possible. He needed to see with his own eyes what they were up against, and he needed to clear his head.

The corner of his mouth tugged up thinking of how he called Syd his fiancé. The look on her face made it all worth it. Playing the part had been even more fun, especially making that sorry excuse of a Sheriff jealous.

He shook his head. That guy was in on it alright. He

had a snaky feel to him and an over-confidence that comes with playing with the big dogs. What did Syd ever see in that guy to call him a friend? Maybe he had been different when they were young. Power could ruin some people.

When he had awakened to Syd loudly telling Wil to leave, the sleep had cleared his head instantaneously. He almost came running out with no pants on, but at the last minute grabbed then, and just in time. That slimy guy had his hands on Syd.

The world had turned red then, and he had no idea what held him back, but it felt like training. It must have been years of training to keep that rage contained. Even with that control, he almost lost it looking down on that slime ball that had thought he could take advantage of his Syd. His. He shook his head. He had no more right calling her his than that dirty Sheriff did.

With the way that Wil had looked at him, Jameson knew he had put things together. Something would happen now. He could feel it in the way his hairs stood up on the back of his neck and the heaviness that lay in the air. Danger had arrived.

At that moment, Jameson froze. Fifty yards in front of him, a man leaned against a lodge pole pine. He wore a sleazy smile while he watched Sydney through the trees while she worked in the goat pen.

Jameson's blood boiled. He clenched his fists and blew out his breath. All he wanted to do was smack that disgusting look off the man's face. He leaned his head into the tree and closed his eyes. It wasn't fear that pulsed through him. It was a need for action, a familiar pulsing that made him feel at home. He let it wash over him until he could focus on what had to be done.

Right now, the sleaze ball needed to remain unaware of his position, and Jameson needed to see how many more were out there. It only took him another twenty minutes of covert movements to find another in the woods across the way, and one more across the driveway.

Jameson breathed to slow his heart rate and thought. Right now the men collected intel. Their guns were holstered or stuck in their pants. They stood relaxed with a lazy air. This meant they had time, and maybe, just maybe, they wouldn't recognize him. He had to give the faux relationship a chance to work, but more than anything, he needed to get Syd inside and safe.

~*~

Sydney finished checking on the new kids and left the barn with a smile. All four were healthy as could be and their mamas too, something that didn't always happen. The sun sank close to the horizon, and she ran through a mental list of dinner options. She wasn't used to so much food being consumed this quickly. A trip to town would be in order soon, but could they swing it?

The sound of boots pounding the dirt made her look up to see Jameson jogging towards her. His furrowed brows and tight shoulders told her something was amiss, which made his words all the more surprising.

"Hey Sweetie!" He called out, plastering on a tight grin. "You finished too? Want to join me in the shower?"

Heat filled her cheeks as he wrapped his arm around her, turning her back towards the house. Her body ignited in a full-on inferno. She opened her mouth, but she couldn't figure out how to address the perplexing scene.

Jameson leaned in close, his lips brushing her neck, sending waves of electricity to her toes and back. She nearly stumbled from the sensation. Jameson's grip on her tightened and his tense, whispered words caused her knees to wobble for a whole different reason. "We are being watched. Three men. Two in the woods and one across the driveway."

She started to turn her head to look back.

"Don't look!" he whispered urgently. "Just follow my lead until we get into the safety of the house."

Her knees buckled then. Jameson swooped her up into his arms, planting a kiss on her forehead. He easily climbed the few stairs up the porch and onto the deck. She couldn't help but think of the significance of crossing the threshold as they entered the house. That's where the charade ended though. He set her down right inside the doorway and pushed her up against the wall, one hand by her head.

"Where's your gun?" His whispered words were rough and urgent.

"One's in the bedroom…" she started in that direction.

"What's the hurry?" he asked in a normal tone. "Can't wait to get into that shower?" Then he bent to nibble her neck again and whispered. "Stay close, don't move from my side."

His eyes swept the room as he shut the front door and locked it. He pulled her up behind him as he peered over the counter, under the kitchen table, behind the couch, and then they slinked down the hall. He toed open the bathroom door before easing in, checking behind the door and then the shower curtain. Then he shut the door and turned on the water.

"Where are the slugs?" he whispered.

"Slugs?"

"The bullets for your shotgun."

"Oh." Sydney's mind swirled, and she steadied herself in Jameson's gaze. "Closet, top shelf. There's a rifle there too, and a handgun in my top right dresser drawer."

Jameson's eyebrows shot up.

She shrugged. Living out in the middle of nowhere, a girl had to be prepared. She remembered Uncle Joe teaching her how to use each gun and the purpose of each different type of firearm. Hunting had never been her favorite thing to do, but she knew how if needed and that was what was important.

"Keep the door closed and locked. I'll knock three times and call your name, otherwise don't open it." Jameson's serious gaze captured hers.

Her heart hammered, and she was sure her eyes looked

as big as saucers.

"It will all be alright, Syd." He took her shoulders in his large hands, gazing calmly down into her eyes. He was focused and intense, but calm. She didn't know those emotions could exist at the same time. His lips brushed against her forehead, and then he opened the door. "You get started, Sweetie. I just need to grab something."

Sydney quickly locked the door behind him before resting her ear against the wood. Adrenaline pricked through her as the small bathroom filled with steam. She could hear doors being slammed open, some rummaging around in the bedroom, and then the sounds of cartridges being clicked into place. Three light knocks sounded on the door.

"It's me, Syd."

She quickly unlocked the door and he rushed in, closing it behind him.

"The house is secure for now. Guardian isn't barking either."

"Are you sure you saw them?" Her eyes searched his. It wasn't that she didn't believe him. She just didn't want it to be the truth.

"Certain." His eyes met hers. "Three males. Two medium built. One large."

"Should we call Wil?" Her nose scrunched up with the thought. It had only been a few hours since he had tried to make a move on her.

"I..." Jameson looked down and then back at her. "Don't you wonder why these guys showed up when they did?"

It took her a moment to process what Jameson suggested. She took a step back. No. Wil couldn't be involved in something like this. Sure, he was an adulterous jerk, but organized crime? She shook her head.

"It's something we have to keep in mind, Syd." Jameson's voice gentled, taking on the horse-whispering tone again. A thick finger smoothed a strand of her hair back behind her ears. "We're going to get through this."

She nodded, wishing she could think more about the real and dangerous predicament they were in rather than the sensation of electricity ripping through her with Jameson's every touch.

He pulled his shirt off in one swift motion, leaving her staring at his naked torso. Her mouth hung open. Then he unbuttoned his pants. Reaching past her, he took a towel and wrapped it around his neck. Somehow his eyes never left hers the entire time.

He then looked away long enough to dip his head in the running shower water. When stood in front of her again, he rubbed his wet hair with the towel and little droplets ran down his smooth chest.

Sydney couldn't breathe. Her heart raced and her mouth went dry. What was he doing? Her body betrayed her as she reached a hand out to touch his rock hard chest. His skin seared her fingers, jolting her back into the situation. Three men lurked outside her house and all because of this man standing shirtless in the steamy bathroom.

Jameson pulled up the hand gun, checked the bullets and cocked it. "Now I look like I rinsed off. You stay here while I do one more sweep."

She nodded.

Moments later, he knocked on the door and called her name. It had given her the time to get her body back under control.

He reached in and turned the shower off. Then he handed her the shotgun. He held the rifle in his other hand. "The house is still clean."

"The men?"

"No signs. Guardian is curled up in his normal spot on the porch. There's no movement indicated." He searched her eyes and then led her to the couch. "I know this is a lot to take in."

"Then why do you seem so calm?" she asked him, her

eyes narrowing.

He shrugged and ran his hand over his head. "It all feels familiar. Too familiar."

"You're a cop." She nodded, doing her best to believe the statement was true. "I don't know what type, but definitely some type of cop. The question is, why were you left for dead on the side of the road?"

"That is the million dollar question, isn't it?" He graced her with a one-sided grin that melted her heart and had her scrambling to remember what they were up against.

# ~10~

Jameson had insisted that Sydney sleep in her bed rather than the cramped couch as he stood watch in the living room. He had double checked all the windows, drawn the curtains, and walked her to the bedroom. He checked the window, under the bed, and in the closet before telling her goodnight.

He heard her tossing and turning. His stomach clenched. The poor lady was enduring this fear because of him. Eventually, she stilled, and he sighed with relief that she was able to get some rest.

It didn't last long though. Chills ran down Jameson's spine as she let out a scream. He was in her room in less than two seconds. Nothing moved in the room besides Syd who quivered in bed, mumbling, and twitching.

"Syd, Syd." Jameson kept his voice calm and soothing as he brushed the hair from out of her face.

She fought to open her eyes, and when she did, they opened wide. He could see the fear ripping through her as her body shook.

"You screamed," Jameson soothed her. "It was just a dream. You're safe."

She blinked a few times before closing her eyes again and nuzzling into the hand he let rest on her head. Soft light poured in from the hallway. Only a glow from the moon snuck under the curtain. His heart ached to bring her into his arms, to promise her he would keep her safe. Instead, he caressed her hair and murmured soothing sounds.

Once she seemed to calm, he reluctantly pulled his hand away and shifted to stand off the bed. As he moved,

Syd's hand shot out and grasped his arm.

"Please stay. I don't want to be alone." Her words were mumbled and her eyes never opened, but her grip didn't loosen until he agreed and lay on top of the covers next to her. A lesser man would use this for his advantage, but Jameson just felt warmth. Knowing that he made her feel safe meant everything to him.

~*~

The rooster crowed for the second time and Sydney grudgingly opened her eyes. Sunlight eased from under the curtains. She scrunched her eyes tight before stretching. When her hand hit something warm and giving, she froze. A body lay next to her…in her bed. Her heart hammered as memories flooded her.

She quickly pulled the blanket up around her tank top and scooted away from the man. He lay atop the covers, fully dressed. Her eyes followed his socked feet, jeans, untucked shirt, and now bearded face. Why was Jameson in her bed?

"Good morning," he said even though his eyes still looked closed.

"What are you doing in my bed?"

"You were having nightmares." He opened his eyes and leaned up on an elbow. "Don't you remember asking me to stay?"

Her eyes narrowed as she tried to sense any deception. A few blurry memories tried to come together, but all she remembered were Jameson's soothing words and caresses. Heat filled her cheeks. Maybe she *had* asked him to stay.

"Now that you're awake, I'm going to do a perimeter check." He fled from the room as if it were on fire.

Sydney hastily pulled on a sweatshirt and pants and then snuck into the bathroom. The cool water on her face didn't ease the heat in her cheeks when she thought of Jameson sleeping next to her. How could she have asked him to stay? Yet, it did show a trustworthiness about him that he hadn't tried anything, right? She knew the last two losers she dated would have used that excuse in a heartbeat.

Mr. Paws scratched at the door and meowed. Poor kitty had been neglected these last few days with everything going on. She opened the door and gave him a few pets, talking to him until he incessantly meowed his need to be fed.

The morning sounds of the ranch mollified Sydney. It made the situation seem more like some bad television movie rather than real life. After feeding Mr. Paws, she started a pot of coffee. Jameson quietly slipped back into the house and locked the door.

"All clear." He peeked out the curtains one more time like he didn't believe it to be true.

"I have to feed." It was a statement, but said like a question because she had no idea what protocol she should be following. The truth was that she started to feel annoyed by the hassle the situation added to her peaceful life.

"I need to use the bathroom, and then I'll head out with you."

She nodded. Her head swam with so much that she had to shut down in order to not get lost in the whirlwind of emotions and stories playing out in her mind.

Just as she poured coffee into two mugs, Guardian began barking, not his normal, *Where you at? I'm hungry* bark, but his intruder alert bark. Gravel popping under tires stopped her heart. Could Wil be coming back again? That would be three days in a row, and after yesterday's altercation, she didn't think she would see him for some time.

Jameson's warm breath stirred her hair. He had somehow snuck up behind her without her hearing him. They walked together towards the window, and with his back against the wall, he eased the curtain out just a fraction of an inch. Sydney leaned over him to get a look as well. Parking in the driveway was a dark SUV.

She sucked in a breath and her heart jump-started in a frantic rhythm.

The door of the car opened and a sharply dressed man eased out, scanning her property as if he was just enjoying a stay at a country resort. The man tugged on his jacket and set his eyes on the house. The door to the SUV stood open and movement shifted inside of it.

"Four suspects. Two in back. One in the passenger seat. The other approaching the house." He had his professional tone again, proving again that he had law enforcement background.

"What are we going to do?" she asked, trepidation lining her voice.

Guardian's barks turned into a menacing growl. The man froze where he stood.

"You meet him exactly like you met me." Jameson handed her the shotgun. "I will be right here, my sights aimed on his heart." He loaded a bullet into the rifle's chamber and aimed it out the window, not even stirring the curtain.

Sydney tried to swallow as her fingers tightened around the cold steel.

Jameson leaned over and unlocked the door. "Stay inside," he whispered.

The shotgun settled into the calloused spot against her shoulder, and she stared at the door. A moment of irony distracted her, thinking of how just a few days ago she stood here in the same position, her gun pointed at a stranger on her property. Now she once again had the gun's sights on a man, this time to keep that first stranger hidden.

Her eyes shot to Jameson quickly. Why was it that he didn't feel like much of a stranger anymore? Could a few days working together really tell her what kind of man he was?

He nodded as if she had spoken aloud, a look of confidence filling his eyes.

With a deep breath, Sydney swung the door open and glared at the stranger through the screen. "That's far enough," she shouted out, doing her best to quell the fear threatening to tremble her voice.

The man's hand spread out in the universal sign of peace. A smile snaked across his trimmed-bearded face. "I come in peace." His accent placed him as not from this area, something east coast maybe.

Jameson stiffened beside her, and Sydney fought to keep from glancing at him.

"What for?" she asked, never taking the gun's sights off of him.

"Now, is this how you greet all of your guests, ma'am?" His condescending tone bristled her ego.

"I don't get many visitors, and yes, unknown men always get this welcome, every time."

The man laughed, a genuine belly laugh. "I like your spunk, ma'am."

"Why are you here?" She took a step closer to the door, causing the gun to push the screen out just enough to let out a squeak. Guardian picked up his menacing growl.

Jameson whispered urgently, "Don't go out there."

"Is your husband home?" The man lowered his arms.

Sydney's mind whirred with responses, but once again the lie popped right out her mouth. "My fiancé is still sleeping."

"Why, that's mighty sweet of you, letting him sleep while you are up and working already."

"I'm a morning person." She shifted the gun against her shoulder, the weight tiring her arm. "Why do you want him?"

"I'm just looking for an old friend that I heard might be around these parts. I thought maybe your fiancé might have seen him."

"He's new around here so I don't think he can help you. Now if you don't mind, I would like you to leave."

"Of course, ma'am." He nodded. "Maybe we can stop by a little later on, once your fiancé is awake?"

"Like I said, he's new around here. Why don't you go talk to Sheriff Whitmore? If anyone can help you find your friend, it'd be him."

"Sure, Sheriff Whitmore," he said the name with a smirk that sent a shiver down her spine. "I'll see you around, ma'am."

The man ambled back to the SUV, giving a final wave before shutting the door and slowly driving back down the gravel drive. Guardian humphed before lying back down on the porch. The gun fell from her arms, its weight too much to hold a second longer. When the dust had settled, she turned to meet Jameson's eyes.

Intensity burned under his furrowed brows. He looked as if he were processing something. She wanted to hear that she had done a good job, because she knew she had. Disappointment and resentment filled her when he said nothing. She slammed the door and went back to her coffee which now had to be warmed back up.

Here she was putting herself, her life, her ranch on the line to hide this man, this stranger, and he didn't even have the decency to tell her *good job*? A fire burned in her chest and her stomach boiled with resentment, or was she just that hungry?

"I know his voice." Jameson's words were said so quietly it took her a moment to fully process them. When she met his eyes again, she realized the importance of what had just transpired. "I remember him, and the memories aren't good." A shudder coursed through his body, it rippled across his muscles.

"What do you remember?" She set the coffee cup down and stood next to him, all annoyance forgotten, well, almost.

"A series of fragmented memories, but he's a ruthless man. He'll do anything to get what he wants."

"He wants you." Her eyes widened.

"I know." He broke eye contact and watched the floor. "We need to get you out of here."

"I need to feed my animals."

"That's the least of your concerns right now, Syd. Don't you get it? That man will not hesitate to hurt you to get to me!" He paced across the room, for the first time not seeming in control. "I don't know if I can take all four, and that's if there aren't more."

The phone rang, interrupting his rant. Her eyes shot to him, and he nodded.

"Hello?" she asked, turning the phone so Jameson could hear as well.

"Hey, Sydney," Homer said, his voice shaky. "There's another of them dark SUVs in my drive now. I, uh, should I still come in? I called Sheriff Whitmore and he told me just to stay inside, that all would be fine."

Jameson met her eyes knowingly.

"Homer, it's Jameson. Those are not men you want to trifle with. Just grab a gun and sit tight. We'll get this figured out soon."

"If you say so, Hotshot. I sure hope you didn't bring all this trouble down onto to Miss Sydney."

"I'm afraid I unknowingly did, Homer, but I won't let anything happen to her. Now sit tight, and we'll get you out of this soon."

"Sure thing," Homer said, not sounding too convinced.

Sydney hung up the phone and stood there staring at it while Jameson paced the living room. An angry energy permeated off of him, guiding her to keep her distance. She had to do something, so she took out some eggs and started breakfast.

"You're cooking breakfast?" Jameson asked a few minutes later, a wry grin spreading across his face.

"I didn't know what else to do." She shrugged, shoving down the emotions that wanted to scream out of her. She couldn't allow herself to really consider the predicament she was in. It seemed surreal, like one of those bad action movies her last boyfriend used to make her watch.

She set a plate full of eggs in front of Jameson who still stood staring at her with a strange expression. What was he thinking?

"Might as well eat. You'll need your strength," she said, nodding towards the food.

He remained standing but inhaled the eggs faster than it took to cook them.

"Thank you." He nodded, that expression still living in his eyes. "I'll make sure you get out of this, Syd. You have my word." The seriousness lining his voice filled her, and she met his eyes.

"I know," she said, simply, and she did. She knew he would do whatever it took to keep her safe.

"I'm going to sneak out the back window. I want you to lock it after me." He checked the chamber in the hand gun as if he had done it a million times before. "I am going to scout the perimeter and see what our options are."

"Are you sure that's a good idea?" she asked, her heart pounding with the thought of him out there with those men, and of being alone without him in the house.

"Not much choice." He locked eyes with her before disappearing over the windows edge and fading off into the forest beyond. Goosebumps raised on her arms. She rubbed them briskly before securing the window and heading back to the kitchen to clean.

~*~

The crisp morning air helped Jameson to focus. That man's voice played in his mind along with snapshots that he couldn't quite process, but the emotions he could. Fear laced through him. Not fear for himself, but for Syd. He brought this ruthless man to her doorstep.

He clenched his fists as he rested behind a tree. The urge to punch the rough bark filled him with intensity. With a deep breath, he kept the urge under control. Breaking a hand would do neither of them any good, especially since his injured shoulder was still not at full strength. He had been able to use it, but he didn't feel he could trust it yet.

Why couldn't he remember anything? His head still hurt, and he tentatively touched the knot that had started to recede above his ear. It would heal. It had to. He had to find a way to apprehend these criminals, all of them, in order to ensure Syd would be safe.

Four men. He might be able to take them all, but could he before one of them got him or Syd? They would use her against him. He knew that. It soured his stomach and he spat into the bush next to him. These men had no morals or scruples. He didn't need a memory to tell him that.

He leaned back out and scanned the woods ahead of him. No movement. Cautiously he made his way from tree to tree until he could see the end of the long drive. Sure enough, a dark SUV sat there. He could see arms moving in heated conversation. Looks like they couldn't agree on the next steps.

He could take this advantage now, sneak up on them and dispatch them. Yet, what if he didn't succeed? What would they do to Syd without him there to protect her?

A sense of helplessness coursed through him. He growled, low and menacingly. It was not a sensation he cared to have, nor did he think he was used to it.

He would have to have Syd call the Bureau. Local law enforcement was out. Thank goodness he had that nagging feeling from the get-go. Yet, maybe it would have been better had he been caught before getting Syd wrapped up in this mess.

Selfishly, he was happy that he had gotten the chance to get to know the strong woman. He of course didn't know for sure, but he felt as if he had never known a lady as capable and yet kind as her.

He glared at the car before easing away through the woods and back to the house, back to Syd.

~*~

The next forty-five minutes felt like forever to Sydney. The animals' normal morning sounds became pleas of desperation. The poor guys were starving, and the mamas needed to be milked. She had to feed them. Guardian harrumphed outside. She snuck him out a bowl of food. At least she could do that.

Pacing back and forth from the kitchen to the window and back again, she wondered if she would completely lose her mind. How could she stay in here and listen to the goats and horses cry for food and not do anything about it? Jameson would be livid if she went out there, and who knows what kind of trouble could be waiting for her.

"Agh!" she screamed, albeit quietly, in frustration.

Mr. Paws looked up at her, jumped off the chair, and ran down the hall. She followed him. He curled up on her bed and she lay next to him, letting her hand stroke his silky fur. It calmed them both. The sound of his purr drowned out the incessant pleas from outside.

Sydney had almost lulled herself into sleep when she heard the three taps on the window.

"Syd, it's me." Jameson's whisper cut through her peace as reality hit her full force once again.

At least he was safe. She quickly unlocked the window and stood back as he clambered in.

Once he was in and the window re-locked, he faced her with a scowl. A smudge of dirt crossed his forehead and cheek. She fought the urge to wipe it off.

"They're keeping surveillance at the end of the driveway. Is going through to Homer's the only other way out?"

"Unless you feel like a ride out the twenty thousand acre BLM land behind my property." She shrugged. It seemed like an option to her. Across the BLM land they would end up in the next county. Sure it could take all day, or longer depending on the horse and the rider, but it would get them out of here.

A few painful cries from the goat barn traveled through the open window. "The milking goats!"

"I did sneak in and feed as much as I could while I was out. Can't the milking wait?"

"No! It's very painful for them and their milk will dry up, along with my major source of income."

Jameson sighed and rubbed a hand down his face. His hands now sported calluses that had started to form over the last few days. "Well, if they were to make a move today it seems like they would have already. It might be better if we acted like all was normal."

He didn't sound too sure, but Sydney wasn't going to argue.

"I do think it's time you made a call though." He lowered his head until it almost rested on his chest.

She had never seen someone look so defeated.

"I wish I was confident I could take them all." He sighed.

"Vigilantism is not going to solve this problem, Jameson," she soothed and placed a hand softly on his arm.

"I just don't know where that call is going to take us...me." He allowed his brilliant green eyes to meet hers. "What if I'm not on the right side?"

"I can't imagine that. You're too moral, and too, well, professional."

His eyes seemed to look deep into her thoughts. "Well, being in a drug gang doesn't seem to fit, but I just can't remember..." He raked his hand across his face, obvious frustration getting a hold of him. "It doesn't matter though. All that is important now is your safety, so the call has to be made."

"To whom though? You may be right about Wil." The thought that Wil could be involved in a crazy crime circle hurt more than she would have thought.

"Well, the sheriff has absolute control in this county. We would have to indicate he's involved with this gang and bring in the Bureau."

"The FBI?" Her heart clenched. This whole situation was too much! How did she get stuck in the middle of some drug gang holdup and needing to call the FBI? She rubbed her forehead and collapsed on the bed.

"You could try the DEA, but what if this really isn't about drugs? We can't trust your sheriff's intel."

"Yeah, I guess you're right." Her heart hammered at the thought of calling the FBI. How did one even go about doing that? It's not like they are listed in the white pages. "Maybe the SUV wouldn't try to stop us from driving out, and we could make it into the next county?"

The expression that covered Jameson's face made her feel quite naïve. "Syd, there's no way around this." He sat next to her on the bed and held his head in his hands. "More memories keep flashing in about that suspect, the one who showed up this morning." He shook his head, pushed himself back up, and began pacing again. "I can't seem to collect them enough to make sense of them."

"It will come." She tried to soothe his distress in order to keep hers at bay.

"Syd, this guy... He's ruthless. Each memory only confirms it." Jameson turned to lock eyes with her, an intense expression filling them. "He won't let us leave."

"Why just sit there? I don't understand."

"They must be waiting for orders…or someone." A horrified expression took over his face.

Her heart raced. Seeing Jameson nervous scared her more than anything else had. Who knew for sure what Jameson did for a living, but his experience in situations like this was clear. He had seemed calm before. Now, his pacing, head rubbing, and sighs made it all too clear: he was nervous.

The goats increased their wailing. The pain lining their cries reminded her of her friend when her baby decided to stop nursing all at once. Her swollen breasts had looked rock hard. She had said it was the worst pain. Those poor goats.

"Is there any long term solution for your milking goats?" Jameson asked, sitting back on the bed.

"Not really. I could see if the kids would nurse from the others, but there really are too many milking goats for the kids to get to them all."

"You will do what I tell you? Immediately, no matter what?" His intense eyes met hers, pulling her into him.

She scooted to the edge of the bed until they sat next to each other, legs touching. "Yes."

He nodded, checked the shotgun, and handed it to her. "Don't leave this out of your reach."

She took the cold steel into her hand. The coolness crept into her skin, crawled up her arm, and sank into the pit of her stomach. Goat farming had always been hard work, but she never knew it would ever be this dangerous.

They walked out to the living room, and Jameson surreptitiously looked out the curtains. When he nodded, she met him at the door.

"Act normal, but stay alert."

Sydney took a deep breath and shook out her hands, before looking up into his green eyes. When he lowered his forehead to hers, a different type of nervousness filled her.

"I'm sorry I brought you into this." His whispered words had hardly left his mouth before he opened the door and greeted Guardian. "Hey boy!" he said as if he had no care in the world.

Guardian jumped around and wagged his tail like he hadn't seen them for a week. She knew the dog sensed the tension going on, but she loved how he could be in the moment. She wished she could follow his lead. He bounded ahead of them, heading straight towards the barn.

With their movement the milking goats rushed over to the fence, bleating their need. Guilt ripped through Sydney. The poor goats had no idea what was going on. They were hurting and in pain because of her, because of her soft spot for a stranger with startling green eyes, large hands, and a physique that left her heart pitter-pattering.

Jameson's eyes scanned the area constantly. Every once in a while they would connect with hers and a softness seemed to reflect there. He opened the gate into the milking corral, and as she entered he wrapped his arm around her shoulder.

"Sorry we made you wait so long ladies!" Then he set his lips so close to her neck his whispered words caused her body to erupt in waves of electricity. "How can I help?"

"You want to learn how to milk?" she teased, not having to fake a smile.

"If it will help this go quicker, absolutely." He nodded, though a corner of his mouth dropped and his eyebrows furrowed.

"Well then, I'll help you get started with Bess here." She handed him a bucket and led him to a brown and white nanny goat. "Okay, first thing we get this girl up on the stand."

She wrapped her arms around the goat and hefted her onto the milking stand. After dumping some grain into the feeding bucket, she handed Jameson the wipes kept in the storage compartment on the side of the stand.

"You have to clean your hands and her teats," she instructed.

"Clean teats, got it," he said with enough amusement that she had to turn to see the glint in his eye she knew would be there.

"Next you place the bucket below her. This bucket is sanitized, and we use a new one for every goat."

He nodded.

"Now, to milk, you wrap your thumb and finger around here." She showed him how to wrap where the teat met the udder. "Then you squeeze. Don't pull." Two squirts of milk sounded in the pail. She looked at the milk and then preceded to show him again. "Got it?"

"I think so. Why'd you look at the milk?"

"To see if there were any impurities like bacteria or other infections."

"Oh," he said, and shifted his weight back and forth, continuing his scan of the land.

"You ready to give it a go?" Sydney asked as she stepped back from the stand.

"Sure," he said, but sounding anything but confident.

Sydney couldn't suppress a smile as she led him to the stand and into position. She took his hand and put it in the correct form. Her hand wrapped around Jameson's felt like touching fire. It shot through her and left her breathless. She shouldn't be feeling this way. This man had so much trouble following him. *How could she let myself fall like this?* She let go of Jameson's hand and backed away from him as if he had burnt her.

"Am I doing it right?" he asked.

"Yeah, great," she said quickly, pushing the feelings down. "Keep that up until she's about dry. You can kind of push here a bit to make sure there isn't more milk in there." She showed him how to put pressure on the utter and then escaped the intensity that being near him caused. Yet it seemed to follow like tendrils teasing her soul. *Focus, Sydney. Focus on milking the goats.*

She tucked back inside the barn to grab another bucket. Coming back out, she ran right into the hard muscled chest of Jameson.

"Oh, sorry," she murmured, her free hand still on his rock hard stomach.

"I told you not to leave this behind," he whispered through gritted teeth.

"I, I forgot." Heat burned her cheeks and fire seemed to scorch her hand. She dropped it rapidly from his hard muscles.

"This isn't a game or something you can forget about." His tone softened somewhat, but still held the hard undertones of anger and fear.

"I know." She blew the hair out her face. How dare he boss her around! "I'm not used to having to protect myself on my own property." She snatched the gun out of his hand and strode off to the next bleating goat.

Out of the corner of her eye, she watched Jameson stand there, back facing her for another moment before slowly making his way back to Bess. She glared in his direction while milking Faun as quickly as possible. Her life was peaceful before he showed up. She had her schedule, her ranch, and her animals. She was fine. She may have been lonely once the nights rolled around, but at least she didn't have to worry about her life or that of her animals.

"Mleah!" Faun looked back at her, protesting the rough treatment.

"Sorry, girl," Sydney soothed and slowed her hands to a normal rhythm.

She took a deep breath, breathing in the smell of Faun and the other goats—the smell of good memories, of times of peace, and love-filled moments. A sigh escaped her as her shoulders slumped. She missed Aunt Mag and Uncle Joe.

Faun's milk ceased and Sydney sent the goat on her way. While traveling to the next nanny, she stopped beside Jameson still fumbling with poor Bess. He tugged gently, too gently, on her teats as droplets of milk dribbled down his large hands.

"Squeeze, don't pull," she directed. "Use those man-hands of yours."

"Doesn't it hurt her, though?" His eyes met hers.

She laughed at his concern over possibly hurting the goat. "No more than getting suckled by a kid."

His brows furrowed even more.

"If you keep that dainty pull up, it'll take you all day to milk her, and make her sore in the process."

"Point taken." He turned his attention back to Bess. "Sorry Bess. Squeeze, don't pull." His new method squirted a good size amount into the bucket. He turned to Sydney with a half-sided grin.

How could she be angry at him when he smiled like that? Her insides turned to mush. She nodded and moved on to the next goat before losing herself in him again.

~*~

Jameson brought the last two buckets into the cheese making room and set them with the others. He stood there, watching Sydney. She moved with such grace even as her arms bulged with the heaviness of the full cans she poured into the cheese making containers.

"I never realized how much work you did every morning," Jameson said as he stretched his hands. "Nothing like a couple of hours of milking to make a guy feel like a weakling."

"It takes a while to build the grip strength." She smiled at him. He loved that smile, so trusting and innocent.

"I guess." He chuckled and shook out his hands. "I sure wouldn't want to play mercy with you."

She looked over her shoulder to peer at him. "I'm not sure how to take that."

His brow furrowed. "As a compliment."

"Not exactly the most feminine quality." She shrugged and picked up another bucket to dump.

"Well, I guess weak women aren't my thing." Somehow he knew that. A pattering of memories flashed through him. Beautiful, flirty women with too much makeup. The emotion that came with the memories were ones of annoyance and lack of connection.

She didn't turn back towards him, but with satisfaction he saw the corners of her mouth twitch. He could get used to a life like this one of hard work and good companionship, with someone like Syd. Who was he kidding? He didn't want a woman like Syd, he wanted her. Should he tell her now, before things went south?

He took two steps toward her, his hand barely grazed her shoulder when he heard it.

The barn door squeaked.

Jameson reacted instantly, his instincts kicking into overdrive. He cocked his gun and pulled Sydney to stand against the wall beside the door. She yanked the shotgun with her and cocked it as well. Admiration for the woman filled him, but he couldn't allow himself to get distracted. He took in even breaths as he waited for the door to fully open.

With his gun squared and ready to fire a chest shot at whoever entered, a familiarity washed over him. This was something he was used to. Something that made him feel at home with who he was. That knowing filled him with confidence as he firmly stood on planted feet.

The first thing to show through the door was a hand, a wrinkled, winter-roughed hand. Jameson's body eased. He lowered the gun slightly and put a steadying hand on the barrel of the shotgun Sydney held aimed at the same spot. She questioned him with her eyes.

"Miss Syd?" Homer whispered as he stuck his head in the door. His eyes went wide when his gaze landed on the guns still loosely pointed at him. "What in tarnation!" he exclaimed.

"What are you doing here?" Sydney ran up and embraced him. "Jameson told you to stay."

"Well, no offense, Hotshot." He eyed Jameson. "I don't know you from a can of beans, even if we have been working together. I needed to know that Syd was safe."

"I respect that." Jameson nodded. "We didn't hear the quad."

"I snuck out the back and walked over." He looked back and forth between the two of them. "Are you going to tell me what's going on, or you going to leave the old man in the dark?"

Jameson shoved the handgun into the back of his pants and did his best to read the old man. Sydney gave him a nod, so he took a breath and blew it out. "Well, I woke up on the side of the road the night before we, uh, met. I had no memory of who I was or how I came to be beat up in the bushes. This place here was the closest house, and Syd was kind enough to let me sleep in the barn."

"You let a strange man stay here?" Homer turned a sharp expression to Syd.

She only shrugged and went back to pouring milk. The lady amazed Jameson. She never stopped working and didn't back down or make excuses.

"So how are you involved in all this mumbo-jumbo?" The older man peered at him with aging eyes.

"Good word. I don't rightly know, but they want me."

"Have you called Wil?" Homer asked.

Jameson watched Syd, she froze in mid-pour and a shudder coursed through her. He wanted more than anything to shield her from that pain and fear. She put down the pail and turned toward the older man.

"He's involved, Homer." Her words were heavy, sad, but spoken with conviction.

"What? No!" Homer shook his head. "He's a good boy. How would he have gotten mixed up with hoodlums like these?"

"I don't know, Homer, but the signs are just too obvious to ignore." She squeezed his arm. Jameson could tell her affection for the older foreman.

Homer furrowed his brows, and Jameson could tell it took a great deal of inner settling before he could wrap his mind around all of this news.

"So, what's the plan?" Homer asked.

Jameson met Syd's eyes, her beautiful multi-colored eyes that he wished he could get lost in rather than face what lay before them. "Syd's going to call the FBI and tell them everything. We'll see what they have to say." He watched the sorrow fill her eyes. Jameson clenched his hands.

# ~11~

Sydney couldn't believe that they had found the FBI's phone number in the phone book. She would have never thought to look there. Jameson had excused himself from the house so she could *talk freely* as he said.

Homer had sat with her, silent and watching.

She hadn't wanted to call the FBI. It sounded absurd to her and yet there was a real danger. She also didn't want to get Jameson in trouble. She had wanted to just leave, escape, but as Jameson maintained, there was no running from a problem like this. It had to be hit head on.

After Sydney gave a brief summary to the first person she was transferred to, she continued to be on hold or transferred several more times. By the time a man with a grizzled voice came on the line, she had left teeth marks in a pencil and torn a sheet of note paper to tiny bits.

"This is Agent Graham. I'm the Special Agent-in-Charge. I hear you have a situation, Miss, uh, Campbell."

"I have explained the situation I don't how many times Agent Graham, and truth be told I didn't want to call in the first place. Do I really have to go through it all again?" She heard the exasperation in her voice and took a breath to steady it.

"No. Your situation has been explained. I just have a couple detailed questions for you." He sounded almost compassionate.

"I'll answer what I can," she sighed, ready to put this nightmare behind her.

"Now you stated this man who showed up at your door with no memory has had a few recollections, including his name, Jameson?" His voice held expectation.

"Yes," she said as her heart raced. She looked out the window for Jameson, a sudden sickening filling her stomach.

"Can you please describe him?"

"Describe him?" A blush crept up her cheeks, and she turned away from Homer's intent attention. "He's well over six feet, broadly built, and has amaz…uh, green eyes. I…I don't want him to get into any trouble."

"Do you know if he has a tattoo with two swords on his upper left arm?" The man's voice held restrained excitement.

"You know who Jameson is?" A lump bobbed in her throat as she held her breath.

"I believe so, Miss Campbell."

"So, you know he isn't dangerous." Was she trying to prove it to him, or herself?

The man laughed, a sound of relief. "Dangerous? If it's the Jameson I think, yes, he's very dangerous, but he will do anything to protect you."

"That's the impression I get." She nodded, her heart easing a bit.

"That's why you need to find a way to leave him if possible."

"Leave him?" Sydney's head raced, how could she leave him here, and where would she go?"

"Do you have a way to hide out somewhere until we can get there?"

"They have all the roads to my property blocked." She didn't want to leave without Jameson. He had become a safety net in the chaos, even if he had brought the problem himself.

"Tell me your address again."

Sydney repeated her address. While she heard the man type away at the computer, a feeling that she couldn't quite decide was relief or remorse coursed through her. This man knew Jameson. The excitement he exhibited sounded like relief and happiness, and he spoke of Jameson with kind familiarity.

"You still there, Miss Campbell?"

"Yes, please call me Sydney," she said. She had never liked being called by her last name.

"Sydney, I see here you butt up to some vacant Bureau of Land Management property. Is there a place there you could hunker down for a night, or even ride through, or connect with a friend's place?"

"There's a cabin at the end of my property. I hadn't thought about it. What about Jameson? Is he one of you?"

Agent Graham chuckled. "Oh, he's one of us. You don't worry about him. He can handle himself. Now if he's distracted by protecting you, that might get messy. These people that are causing you trouble are serious. It would be best for everyone involved if you got to a safe place immediately."

"What about Jameson? When can I tell him you will be here to help?"

"The team is assembling as we speak. We'll be there in a couple hours tops."

"Is there anything else I should tell him? Shouldn't he just come with me? Wouldn't he be safer that way?"

"They would pursue, and like I said, it could get messy. Trust me. Don't you worry about Jameson. Even with amnesia, he's not someone to trifle with. You just get to a safe location. We'll come get you when your home is secured." He paused, and she could hear muttered voices. "I've got to go. The team is ready to head out."

"Okay," Sydney said, still feeling uncertain about everything, especially leaving Jameson alone.

"Oh, and Sydney, thank you for calling. Jameson will be safe because of you, and we will help him recover his memories. We'll see you soon."

The line went dead. Sydney held the phone until the beep-beep-beep sound blared into her ear. She pressed the off button and set it on the table where she collapsed into the chair. Her heart pounded with indecision as she squeezed her eyes shut. She knew she should be running to get her things ready for a stay at the old cabin, but she couldn't wrap her mind around it.

~*~

Jameson slid behind the thick pine that had been his shield for the last couple of days. There were now two SUVs parked at the end of the driveway, the drivers in deep discussion. From his position he could not make out the words, and he couldn't get closer without jeopardizing his position. Tension filled the air in the same way an electrical storm charged the sky before its onslaught.

The attack would soon come.

He needed to prepare. He needed to get Sydney somewhere safe, and Homer too.

Stealthily, he maneuvered through the forest back to the house. He paused at the top of the steps, still doing his best to find a solution that would keep Sydney out of the mess. His fists clenched at his sides. It was his fault she was in the middle of this. He needed to keep her safe.

The screen door squeaked, and he slowly looked up to meet multi-colored eyes full of mixed emotions. He immediately noticed that she had a backpack slung over her shoulder.

"I was right." Her eyes met his, open and trusting. He hoped he lived up to that trust.

"You were right?" he asked, not wanting to breathe, for he knew this might be the last time they saw each other.

"Yes, you're one of the good guys. Agent Graham, does the name trigger anything?"

Memories shot through him so fast he threw an arm out to grasp the railing for support. The barrage gave him a better feeling for who he was, but he couldn't completely access the memories enough to share them. He just knew that it felt right and good.

"I'll take that as a yes." Her voice softened as she took two steps to close the distance between them and laid a hand on his arm.

"Yes, definitely triggers." He watched her small hand on his arm. So small and feminine, yet so strong. Without the power to restrain himself, he took her hand in both of his and brought it up to his lips. He wanted to remember the feeling of her touch and the smell of her skin. "You're leaving. How? Where?"

"When talking with Agent Graham, I remembered an old homesteading cabin at the edge of my property. He said I had to leave you, that you would be safer without me distracting you."

The corner of his mouth lifted as he raised his eyes back to hers. Yeah, she was a distraction, one he would like to have more often. Not today though, today it could mean life or death, hers and his. "It would be safer for you, and I guess for me, if I knew you were in a secure location."

She nodded. He saw her swallow and push her shoulders back. "Do we have time to take the horses?"

"The men at the end of the road are getting ready to act now. You would be faster on horses though." He thought about the trade-off, trying to sense which would be the safer option. "How long would it take you to saddle them?"

"Awhile, but we could ride bareback."

Jameson scanned the yard. The horses were corralled on the opposite side of the driveway which should keep them hidden if they were quick. He nodded. "It has to be done now."

Sydney stiffened, but she nodded and called in to Homer, "You can still ride bareback, right?"

"Yes, Miss Syd. I'm not that old yet." He wheezed out a pathetic attempt for a laugh.

"Then let's go."

"Take Guardian with you. It'll be good for you to have him." Besides, Jameson didn't want the dog getting shot while trying to protect him. He didn't need to say that to Syd though.

She nodded. "Come on, boy," she called the dog to her side. Syd gently pulled her hand from Jameson's and started down the steps before she turned back to him. "The guns and all the ammo I have are on the table. I'm sorry for…" She blinked several times before turning her head and striding towards the corral.

Jameson caught up with her in less than a half dozen strides. He grasped her arm and pulled her into him. Wrapping his arms around her slight frame, he breathed in the scent of her hair, letting the aroma fill him.

Homer continued past them with a sideways glance and softly whistled for the horses.

Jameson loved the way Syd melted into his arms. He squeezed her tighter to him, never wanting to let her go. She fit so perfect against him. Too soon she, seemingly reluctantly, pushed away to look at him, her eyes brimming with unshed tears.

"When this is all said and done, will you, uh," Jameson coughed, and then chuckled nervously. "Will you go out to dinner with me?"

Syd stared at him for a very long moment before laughing and melting back into his arms. "Yes, Jameson. If you find your way back here, I will go out to dinner with you."

He blew out a breath he didn't know he had been holding and rested his head on hers. He wanted to hold her forever, even though he knew it would be safer for both of them for her to go. If it hadn't been for the charged air and imminent danger about ready to strike around them, he wouldn't let go of her. He kissed her forehead, then her temple, along her jaw, and her chin.

Her mouth parted, her breath matching his and warming him. He met her eyes so close. Her gaze softened before traveling down to his lips, less than an inch from hers. He couldn't stop the momentum they had built up as his mouth crashed down upon hers. He needed to express all the emotions he could never find words for.

As their lips mingled, his heart tugged and ached, and his stomach filled with flutters. He didn't know what love felt like, and thought it too soon to know of such things anyway, but what he did know was that he was falling for the gal who had saved his life, in more ways than one.

~*~

Sydney couldn't believe she was kissing Jameson. When she had realized what his intention was, all she could do was follow it. Once their lips touched, the rightness filled her to the core. She had kissed men before, but none held so much power, so much force that the air rushed out of her lungs and yet filled her at the same time.

His large hands threaded through her hair. His scent filled her. His lips devoured her, and yet it felt as if his soul had opened up, inviting her in, coaxing hers to meet his. Tingles swept through her in a rush of butterfly-like flutters.

No, she had never been kissed like this.

She knew love, or what she thought love was, but she couldn't rightly call this love so soon, right? Yet, she knew as soon as he pulled away and she rode off across the land, her heart would break from loss. Even if everything turned out fine after this mess, she couldn't be with someone who worked in the FBI. That was a life of danger, and she couldn't handle this level of adrenaline on a daily basis.

She pulled him into her, wanting to give all she could, knowing that it most likely would be the last time, knowing she probably would never be kissed like this again and that no other man would ever be able to compare.

Homer cleared his throat.

Syd grudgingly pulled away, her soul screaming at her. She rested her head against Jameson's as they both panted with more than physical exertion. Looking in his eyes, she knew he felt the intensity too. It was no ordinary kiss.

"The cabin is due south, hit the fence line and go west until the valley opens up, and you'll see it." She rushed out the words, pulled him to her for a brief second, and then quickly pushed away. She flung her leg over the gelding that Homer held for her. "Agent Graham said they'd be here within a couple hours. Please stay safe until then."

"I will. I'm a man of my word, and I promised you a dinner." Jameson's sideways grin about cut through her grit and had her slipping off the horse and back into his arms.

If it wasn't that Graham said it would be safer for him, she would have argued and stayed put. She couldn't see Jameson hurt though. She returned to her horse.

"I'm holding you to that, Cowboy," she said, before lifting her hand in a final farewell and kicking the horse into a trot away from the corral, away from her land, and away from her unexpected cowboy.

# ~12~

Jameson's mind swam. With the mention of Graham, his mind hadn't rested. Without Syd here to distract him, the memories solidified, becoming more tangible. Loading the guns and preparing the house for a siege became methodical. This wasn't the first time he had held off a group of men on his own.

At least he knew the cavalry would arrive soon. He hoped soon enough. He had a promise to keep.

The noises of the ranch came to him through the windows. He missed the comfort of the shaggy dog on the porch. Guardian's keen sense would have warned him as danger approached. Jameson would have never had forgiven himself if something had happened to that loyal animal though. The dog was Syd's constant companion and protector.

"Meow." The cat rubbed up against his leg.

He reached down and picked up Mr. Paws, scratching him behind the ears. "Now, when it gets loud you follow your instincts and find a good hiding place."

The cat purred his response. Jameson smiled. Here he was talking to the animal just as Syd would do. Somehow it comforted him. He wondered if that's why Syd did it, or if it came naturally from spending so much time alone. Being alone felt familiar to him, too.

If he was to live past this, he planned to rectify that for both of them. He and Syd belonged together. He knew that more than he knew his past, and he didn't care what memories surfaced. That feeling of belonging wouldn't be swayed.

The animals started to practically yell in a frantic

clamor. Jameson's heart picked up its pace. He gave the cat a final scratch and then closed it into the bathroom. Flush against the wall, he made his way back to the living room. His head hit a picture, but he caught it before it fell to the ground.

All at once, he wished he had thought to make his stand out in the forest rather than Syd's house. As quickly and quietly as possible, he took the pictures off the wall and set them on her bed. If bullets came flying through the windows he didn't want her photos to be ruined.

He snuck back out to the front of the house, rifle in hand. Pulling the shades back ever so slightly, he scanned the area. The goats ran around in their pens, acting as nervous as if a storm was approaching. In a way it was. He blew out a breath.

They were out there. The question was where.

A dark SUV slowly rolled down the drive. Jameson snorted. The audacity of this guy. So this was how he would play this. Jameson eyes shifted to the clock on the microwave. He had at least a half hour or more until Graham arrived. Then it would depend on protocol. Would his old friends just fly and drive in with a rush or go stealth and pick off the perps on their way in?

Familiar memories rushed through him. If his instincts and flashes of memories were right, Graham would go stealth. Gratitude filled him for the man who would be coming to his rescue. The more memories that filtered in, the more he realized that this man was more than a boss, but a good friend too.

The SUV pulled to a stop about twenty yards from the house, close enough to get shots in, but far enough they could mostly stay hidden behind the doors. It sat there, taunting him while he held his breath. Then he blew it out. Let them call the shots on how this started. Let them take their time.

Jameson's game plan was all about stalling anyway. He needed this man alive. He was the key to the head of the organization. Jameson could see the reports he had studied. Though he couldn't remember everything, some things had been drilled in him enough that he knew them. Why he had been flung from the car and beat still eluded him, but it seemed this guy and he had a history. This man had a bone to pick with Jameson.

The driver's door slowly opened. A moment later the same man stood behind it, tugging down his coat and scanning the ranch just as he had the first time he stopped, as if things weren't about to go down, as if he weren't preparing for an all-out war to get what he wanted. The man's eyes seemed to meet Jameson's through the slat he peeked through.

Jameson held himself with a hand on the wall as more memories flashed through him. O'Neal.

Jameson ground his teeth. He aimed the rifle right at O'Neal's head. It took all of his willpower not to just take the shot and end this whole thing right now. Taking in a slow breath, he pushed it back out, doing his best to calm his heart rate, and to let emotions go. This was a job, and they needed that scoundrel for questioning. If they could get to the head of this organization, they had the chance to end the drug distribution in small towns all across several states.

The cocky snake took a few steps around the SUV towards the house.

"Hello there, Jake...though that's not how you introduced yourself to me, now was it?" The man called out in a loud booming voice, confirming Wil's involvement. That would be the only way he knew the made-up name Syd gave him.

Familiarity sparked in Jameson. He knew O'Neal, what he did, what he was known for, but though he had a feeling he had interacted with him, specific memories with the weasel eluded him. Jameson must have been undercover. That felt right. It also would explain how he ended up in the bushes. He was lucky he still lived.

"You know loyalty is everything to us. Imagine our surprise when we found out that the man who had let us down back in the capitol also happened to be FBI. Our own man." O'Neal shook his head. "Now what do you have to say for yourself?"

Jameson wanted to show him what he had to say. Instead he clenched his teeth and squeezed the rifle in a white-knuckled grip.

"I see. You're too ashamed to say anything. I would be too." O'Neal looked around the ranch, took a few steps closer to the house. "I had wondered why you had stayed here. Thought you Bureau boys had protocol to follow. Then I saw her. She's pretty and spunky too."

Jameson tensed. Every muscle in his body threatened to crush his own bones. He forced himself to breathe. Syd was safe. By now she would be hunkered down in the cabin, probably bored stiff. Then he smiled. She probably was scrubbing that cabin until it shone. That gal couldn't sit still to save her life.

"I'm looking forward to seeing her again. I bet you'll feel like talking then, won't you?"

Jameson knew the game he played, but he wouldn't be able to hold her against him. She was safe.

"Oh, you don't know." The tone of O'Neal's voice immediately stiffened the hairs on the back of Jameson's neck. "My men saw her and the old man take off on the horses. They're following her trail now. It might take my men awhile since they're afoot, but don't worry, she'll be joining our party soon."

The world turned red as Jameson panted and growled in frustration. Everything in his body wanted to storm out the house, firing rampantly into the cocky snake threatening Syd. His rational brain, though, eventually won out. He knew the trap O'Neal attempted to snare for him.

Once Jameson calmed down, he rationalized, wondering if he could sneak out the back window and catch the men before they found Syd.

"I bet right now," O'Neal said as he inspected his nails, "you're thinking of trying to run after her. I wouldn't. I have men surrounding the house. If you show your face anywhere but this front door right here, they have shoot-to-kill orders."

The growl started low in Jameson's throat. He lifted his fists, bringing them down to smash the table. He caught himself just in time, remembering the way Syd lovingly ran her hands along the worn-smooth wood. He paced back and forth out of the windows' views. *Come on, Graham. I need you here now before I take out our only lead.*

It became eerily quiet for too long. Jameson finally became aware of that fact and snuck a glance through the window. O'Neal discussed something with one of his men in hushed and heated tones. Then he spoke into a radio. O'Neal's face turned red and scrunched as he spoke through his teeth into the radio.

Hope sparked within Jameson. Maybe Graham had arrived and were taking out the perimeter men. As if on cue, a slight reflection from near the barn caught his attention. The flash continued in a repeated pattern. The meaning clear to Jameson.

The cavalry had arrived.

"What do you mean the men have been taken out? You said he was in the house. Burn it down then, and find him!" O'Neal screamed at the man next to him who hurriedly grabbed a gas can from the car.

Jameson thought quickly. He shoved the handgun into the back of his pants and flipped his shirt over it. He positioned the rifle against the inside of the front door for easy access if he had to rush back in for defense. The idea of walking out there into the open didn't sit well with him, but he had to keep them from burning the house.

With his hand on the door knob, he took a deep breath. It seemed like only hours before when Syd was in the same place, breathing deep before meeting the snake that stood out there now. Yet, this time was different. This time he knew the dangerous situation he was in.

Jameson swung the door open just as a man with a gas can walked onto the porch. The man's hands were full and cumbersome. He dropped the can, but not quickly enough. Jameson acted with instinct. He took two strides to the man, grabbed his arm and spun it around behind him and up.

The man grunted in pain and Jameson twisted it a tiny bit more to make the point clear. He was his.

"I'm here, O'Neal." Jameson's voice boomed over the ranch, as he pushed the man down the steps in front of him, never letting go of his arm and keeping his other hand to hold the pistol at the guy's temple.

O'Neal spun around at the sound of Jameson's voice. He quickly sized the situation up and then nodded.

"You were always good, Jake. I should have known you would acquire collateral to help keep your lady friend from harm."

"Don't you talk about her. Call your men off."

"Oh, you know I can't do that now." He took a few steps towards Jameson and the man he held hostage. "Now, Doofus Dave, why did you get yourself caught like that. If you weren't my nephew I'd out you myself."

Jameson knew he took that risk. O'Neal was known for being ruthless, even with his own men. In fact, even if the guy under his gun was the man's nephew, when it came down to the line, Jameson knew O'Neal wouldn't hesitate to kill the guy.

Jameson slowly walked Dave towards his uncle as O'Neal took a few steps to meet them.

"So, as you see here, Jake, we have a predicament. I promised my sister I would keep her son safe, and it seems you promised to keep that nice lady safe."

"I'm sure we can reach some arrangement." Jameson's words came through clenched teeth, every fiber of his being primed for what he knew he had to do. Just two steps closer. "Call your men off," he said each word emphatically.

"Now, now, we've been over this."

Jameson shoved the pistol harder against Dave's head and pulled his arm up tight enough it made the man whimper. "Now."

"Okay, okay." He took another step towards Jameson. Just one more.

O'Neal lifted the radio to his mouth. "Jenkins, status."

"We've picked up their trail heading west at the fence line."

O'Neal met Jameson's gaze, a dark expression coming into his eyes. "You know what to do."

"Yes, sir," the radio crackled.

Jameson ground his teeth as he tightened his hold on the man's nephew.

"You see, Jake. I can't let you go. It would be signing my death certificate." O'Neal's arm slowly dropped lower.

Jameson saw the glint of metal under O'Neal's jacket. O'Neal caught his gaze, dropped the radio and reached for the gun. Jameson took that last step, shoved Dave to the ground, turned his pistol towards the O'Neal. He could shoot him right here and be done with it, but instead he pulled back and side cocked the snake on his temple. O'Neal went down, slumping on top of his nephew.

Jameson kicked the gun that fell from O'Neal's hand and kept the pistol aimed down at the two men who lay unmoving. He scanned the area. His eyes caught movement at the barn. A man in a black mask, the man who had been flashing before, came out, gun and eyes scanning as well. He nodded towards Jameson, and then touched the black device at this throat.

"Area secured."

Relief swept through Jameson as the man lowered his gun and cuffed the two men at his feet.

"Good work, sir," the man in black said, as he pulled up his mask. The guy's face was familiar but Jameson couldn't come up with a name.

"Good timing," Jameson said as he eyed the dozen other men in black appearing from behind the house, the barn, and the forest to meet them.

One in particular strode straight towards him, he lifted his mask and smiled broadly.

Graham.

Jameson grinned.

"You always know how to make a show, Jameson." Graham came up to him and pulled him into a rough hug before slapping him on the back. "What's all this?" He tugged at the scruff on Jameson's chin. "I guess I'll let it pass since you've been undercover." He laughed.

With seeing Graham's face and hearing his voice and laugh, a rush of memories flooded Jameson. He stumbled slightly with overwhelm. Bending over, he grasped his knees in order to not fall. Jameson's head swam.

"Hey man, you alright?" Graham nudged him gently.

"Yeah, just…my memory is coming back. It's a lot to take in." He drew in a deep breath and unsteadily stood upright, a hand on his head.

"You've led quite the life." Graham stood back, watching him without expression.

"So it seems." Jameson growled. There were many things he wished had remained forgotten. What he did know was that he was in need of a career change. That life no longer suited him. Besides, Syd would never be okay with him slogging off to dangerous work all the time. "Syd!"

"Yes, she's in a safe location." Graham stated.

"Didn't you hear him? He sent his men after her. I have to go." Jameson looked around wildly. The quad would have been the fastest, but that was all the way over at Homer's. Their trucks wouldn't make it out there. His eyes landed on the red roan. The horse looked lonesome in the corral all by himself.

Jameson rushed out the directions to the cabin to Graham and then opened the corral gate. A halter hung on the fence post there and he grabbed it. He called the horse over to him, haltered him quickly, swinging the lead rope around for reins as he saw Syd do. With a deep breath he grabbed its mane and threw a leg over the back of the horse. If he had ever ridden bareback before, it hadn't been since he was a child, but there was no time to saddle now. He gripped the horse's side with his knees and leaned forward.

"Let's go catch your friends." He clucked his tongue.

The horse didn't need any further coaxing. He took off, quick to trot and then canter. Jameson held on for his life, his shoulder burning and knee aching. It didn't matter though. He had to get to Syd before those men did.

He made it to the fence line, and the horse turned west on his own. Jameson's muscles fatigued and he felt his grip loosening on the smooth muscles underneath him. It wouldn't do Syd any good if he fell off now. He gritted his teeth and clenched tighter. Almost there.

The cabin came into view, looming in a clearing behind a stand of trees. Jameson's eyes bounced as the roan galloped toward his friends tied at a hitching post. It was hard to focus, but he saw two men, one at the side window, the other rounded towards the front of the cabin out of sight.

The sound of hooves pounding the earth must have caught the attention of the man by the window. He stood out in the path of the horse, his gun aimed. Jameson grunted with effort as he dug his heels into the horse's side. They plowed right into the man, who spun, hit his head on side of the house, and fell.

Jameson didn't stop to see if he still moved. He clung to the horse and guided him around to the front of the house. The man there turned abruptly at the sound of his approach and raised a gun, pointed right at Jameson.

Jameson launched himself at the man from horseback right as the sound of gunfire broke the air in a loud, reverberating blast. Pain propelled into his shoulder, fire laced through his ribs, but he and the man he had landed on remained still.

~*~

Sydney dumped the full dustpan outside for the third time. As she closed the flimsy door, her breath caught. There was movement at the tree line. At her side, Guardian growled. She closed the door and moved to the window, pulling the dog close. Goosebumps broke out on her skin and she shook.

"Syd?" Homer questioned.

She slammed a finger to her lips, her eyes wide and heart pounding. Homer tiptoed over to her, handing her a gun and peering out the window.

"I hope Hotshot was worth it," Homer grunted.

Her heart pounded with what might happen, but then she thought of never meeting Jameson. A part of her believed that whatever happened, it was worth knowing him. Besides, he promised to keep her safe. From what she knew of him, he wasn't one to break those promises.

Unless...

She shook her head. She couldn't afford to even think of what these men being here might mean for Jameson.

"Should we shoot on sight?" Homer whispered.

Syd shook her head. What if they were Graham's men coming to tell them it was safe to return? She peeked out the window again. These men weren't dressed like she thought the FBI would dress. They looked like slicked-back cowboys to her.

Sydney and Homer stood against the wall on either side of the only door to the small cabin not that these walls would hold back any bullets. She could see light streaming in from between the boards. A shadow crossed the window to her right. Her heart raced as she leveled the gun at the window.

At first she thought the thundering sound was her heart, but soon she realized it came from beyond the walls and took on the distinct rhythm of a horse in full gallop.

Jameson.

Tingles rushed down her spine and her heart thundered. He had come for her!

She met Homer's eyes that crinkled in knowing as he nodded.

The grunts out the window and the sound of flesh against the wall left Sydney's stomach queasy. The sound of horse hooves then rounded the house. When she heard the gunshot behind her, she doubled over with a sickening feeling. It only grew worse with the deathly silence that followed the blast.

Guardian barked, frantically pawing at the door. Without thought, she grasped her gun and swung the door open.

Her red roan pranced away to stand with the other horses. A groan sounded near her feet. Guardian whimpered and nudged at the bodies lying there. Jameson lay on top of another man, his breathing rapid and shallow.

"Jameson!" She knelt down beside him, touched his face and watched his eyes flutter open.

"Syd. You okay?" His green eyes were dark and unfocused.

"Yes, we're fine. Thanks to you." Her hands brushed over his hard muscled body in search of wounds and came back bloody. "You're hurt!"

"Just a scratch. It's nothing." His tight voice told her he wasn't telling the truth. "Homer?"

"I'm here, Jameson." The older man stood in the doorway, still as a statue.

"Find something to tie these two up, in case they come to consciousness." He groaned as he uneasily rolled off the guy he had landed on.

A bright red puddle of blood spread across the man's chest, but he breathed. Sydney then turned her eyes towards Jameson lying awkwardly and realized that the blood had come from him. She passed Homer exiting with a roll of twine as she ran inside and shifted through the cupboards until she came up with some sheets. Running out to Jameson, she stuffed the cloth on his wound where the blood surged with each pulse right under the outside of his collar bone.

Using all her strength, she pressed the sheet on his wound while he gritted his teeth and closed his eyes. She freed one hand to brush her fingers along his bearded chin.

"You better hang in there. You promised me a dinner, remember?"

Jameson opened his eyes and chuckled shortly before groaning and grabbing his ribs. "I could never forget."

Sydney bent over and kissed him lightly. His lips turned into a slight smile before his eyes closed as he let go of consciousness.

"Jameson. Jameson!" Sydney called his name. Her hand went to his pulse on his neck and saw that it still beat, and he breathed, although shallowly.

Jameson had only been unconscious for a few minutes when a loud whomping sound filled the sky. It became louder and louder until the wind picked up as the helicopter landed in the clearing behind the cabin.

Guardian barked, around her and Jameson in a frantic dance.

"Homer, would you get him inside please," she asked, raising her voice to be heard over the loud thrumming.

He nodded, grabbed Guardian by the collar, and took him into the house.

A man in his late fifties jogged towards Sydney. His eyes narrowed and never left Jameson lying in her arms. He slowed as he came closer, his eyes moving from the bloody, still form of Jameson to hers.

"He…?"

"He's alive." She met the concerned brown eyes. Even from the one word he spoke, but mostly from the way he reacted to Jameson lying in her arms, she placed him.

"Agent Graham?"

"Yes," he said, lowering to her side to place a finger on Jameson's neck. He turned away from them and yelled, "Bring the stretcher."

"You'll make sure he's okay?" Sydney stared hard at Graham before lowering her eyes to Jameson's. She traced his cheek and wished she could see his beautiful green eyes one more time.

"On my honor," Graham said in a deep serious tone. "Thank you, Sydney, for helping us find him."

She nodded, wishing that the bad guys had never found them and Jameson could have just stayed on the ranch. It wasn't a fair wish though. Jameson needed to know his past, even if it took him away from her.

"It's safe to return home now. Jameson caught O'Neal and his nephew. No one should be bothering you again."

"Thank you," Sydney said, but her thoughts and her eyes were on the man in her arms.

Two men in all black ran up with a stretcher in between them. They looked for her permission before taking the unconscious Jameson off her lap and placing him gently on the stretcher. Sydney brushed her lips on his forehead as they carried him towards the awaiting helicopter. Already an emptiness washed over her.

"Will you let me know...?" Her voice trailed off. She couldn't meet Graham's eyes. Instead she kept them locked on Jameson as they secured him and the stretcher aboard the machine.

"I've seen wounds like this. Lucky for him the bullet seems to have missed any major arteries, and you kept him from losing too much blood. He'll make it, but yes, someone will let you know." Graham nodded and then strode towards Jameson and the awaiting men.

As the helicopter lifted into the sky and disappeared over the trees, she became aware of all the activity still surrounding her. Men were pulling up the two gang members who had come to, cuffing them, and hoisting them to their feet. They would have a long walk back to vehicles at the ranch.

How had Jameson knocked them both unconscious like that? Secretly she was relieved that he hadn't killed them. A shudder traveled through her. The nightmare of the day could have gone much worse. She had Jameson to thank for that, as well as for her life. Her eyes traveled towards where the helicopter had disappeared, and she sent a silent prayer for his recovery.

## ~13~

It hadn't taken too long for life to return to normal on the ranch. Animals still needed to be fed and milked. Cheese and soap still needed to be processed. Repairs still needed fixing.

During the lengthening days, she found herself searching for Jameson out in the fields, but it was at meal times, and especially at night, that her heart ached from his absence. She missed his quiet, observant attention, his intelligent, attentive green gaze, easy-going conversation, and his larger-than-life presence.

At night, she started having Guardian sleep in the house. She put his bed right in front of the door. It gave her peace of mind to have the dog inside. Mr. Paws on the other hand strongly voiced his dislike of the situation.

Today Sydney was introducing the new kids to the outside corral. Brownie gave her a little nuzzle, and it left her heart aching. She would probably never give Brownie up. The little kid always reminded her of the gentle way Jameson took care of her during the kidding.

She watched the kids explore as the sound of gravel popping in her driveway made her heart speed up. Guardian sidled up to her, a low growl in his throat. First tremors of fear filled her, and then hope. She didn't know which was worse.

She checked the weight of the pistol she now carried everywhere with her.

The rough edge of the barn scratched her face as she hugged it, ready to peer around it to see who pulled up to her house. Guardian took a few steps out towards the driveway barking. She peeked around the corner, hating that she had resorted to paranoid thinking. Graham had said she wouldn't be bothered anymore and the rumor mill said Wil had been taken into custody, but who actually knew?

Her heart hammered as she waited for the vehicle to pull up in front of the house where she could see it. The gravel popped before a white delivery van showed itself.

Sydney blew out the breath she didn't know she had held. Heat filled her, both in embarrassment and in self-reproach. She was going to have to get over this. Patting the gun in its holster, she walked around the barn toward the delivery van. About halfway there her steps faltered.

She hadn't ordered anything.

Her hand reached for the gun just as a uniformed delivery guy came out of the back of the van with a book-sized brown box in his hand and a smile on his face. Guardian ran up to the guy who gave him a treat and then ruffed up his head.

"Miss Campbell? Got a package for you." The young man smiled as he steadied his eyes on hers.

Sydney dropped her hand once again. She recognized the delivery man. He had been out a few times before to deliver the meds she had ordered for the goats. Her heart eased a bit as she continued walking towards him.

"I didn't order anything, Sam."

"I don't know where they come from, I just deliver them." He shrugged. "Maybe it's a present."

"Maybe," she said hesitantly while taking the package he handed to her. Maybe her parents finally remembered her birthday.

"Have a great day," Sam said as he hopped back into his truck. "It's starting to get warm."

"It is. Thank you." She waved as he shut his door and turned the truck around to travel back down her long drive.

There was no return address on the box. She turned it all around while walking towards the house. As the steps creaked with her weight, a squeal sounded from the corral.

"The kids," she said, and she dropped the package at the top of the steps and ran towards the corral, Guardian on her heels.

One of the kids hid behind his mom while another nursing mother with an older kid stood in attack mode. Sydney hopped the fence and came between them.

"It's okay, Lucille. This is just another kid to look after." She spoke calmly to the goats going through the drill of introductions. Hopefully damage hadn't been done from her lack of guidance.

The package was forgotten as she returned her focus to her ranch tasks.

It wasn't until dusk began to settle and Sydney made her way back to the house that she saw the package and remembered. Guardian sniffed it, then plodded on to his bed, circled a few times, and plopped down. He looked over at her with lonesome eyes, his head resting on his paws.

The poor dog had moped around since Jameson had left. She wasn't the only one that missed the cowboy.

FBI cowboy. She shook her head. A couple weeks after that crazy day, Agent Graham had let her know that Jameson had recovered. After a couple more weeks of listening intently for the phone or for him to show up, she succumbed to conclusion he wouldn't.

It was probably for the best she hadn't heard from Jameson. Even though her thoughts couldn't let him go, she could never be with him. Her heart couldn't handle always wondering if he was okay and if the job he was on would be his last.

To get her mind off her broken heart, she took the package and sat on the porch swing. Digging in her pocket for her multi-tool, she pulled it out and clicked open the blade. With a quick movement of her wrist she cut the tape along the package before slipping the tool back into her jeans.

"Let's see who sent us something," she told Guardian, but the dog only snored a response.

The package had the smell of cardboard, but as she opened she inhaled the faintest scent of Jameson. She lifted her nose and closed her eyes. It must have traveled on the breeze. Her heart clenched before she closed it off.

Folding back the panels she saw a simple, wooden frame, just like the one Jameson had accidently broken. She sucked in a breath. Her throat swelled and her eyes watered. He remembered. She lifted the frame gently from the box and searched the bottom with her other hand.

No note. Nothing but the frame.

A piece of her heart broke a little more. It was just like Jameson, to return something with no words. A soft smile stretched her lips even as her heart ached.

She nodded. This might as well be his way of saying goodbye. Maybe he knew her enough to know she couldn't be with him with his chosen profession. It would be easier this way than saying goodbye in person...after the date he had promised her.

After slipping off her boots, she took the frame inside, gingerly put Aunt Mag and Uncle Joe's wedding picture into it, and hung it back up in its spot. Seeing it hang there settled the shakiness in Sydney. The frame really did look like the original, just another show of Jameson's observant nature.

Sydney sighed. She had known this would happen. The loneliness she had before was nothing like she felt now with Jameson's massive presence missing. She grabbed a package of goat cheese and some crackers, then sat down to have her dinner.

She smiled thinking of Jameson's large appetite. Eating like this was simple, but she missed having a reason to cook, and the food that resulted from it.

As she snacked silently at her table, she thought about what the grocer had said when she dropped off cheese the day before.

A new sheriff. Her old friend, Wil, had been taken into custody by the FBI for further investigation. A small part of her felt sad that he had allowed himself to be dragged into such a mess, another poor decision on his part.

The gossip grocer talked incessantly about the new sheriff, making sure to tell Sydney this one *was* single, though supposedly his heart was already taken. Sydney had smiled politely. Her heart ached too much to even think about an eligible bachelor new to the county. Her heart was taken too.

With resignation, she put things away to get ready for bed. "Come on, boy," she called to Guardian who happily pranced his way inside. Mr. Paws hissed and ran to the bedroom. "Oh, Mr. Paws, it's not that bad," she said as she positioned the dog's bed in front of the locked door. "Besides, it lets me actually sleep, huh, Guardian?" She scratched his big shaggy head. "Get some rest, boy, it's an early day tomorrow."

On her way to bed she thought with dread about the Mountain Valley Farm Day. She disliked working these events, but her booth always increased her customer base and earned her over a month's revenue in one day.

Once in bed, her mind immediately went to Jameson. She thought of the night he had slept on her bed, fully clothed just to help her feel safe.

She wished he could do so again…

~*~

Jameson sat in the truck at the corner in Syd's driveway, the closest he could get and see the house without alerting her of his arrival. His restless fingers tapped the steering wheel, his foot squeezed the brake.

Her house was awash in lights, a beacon that called to him after his first day on the new job. His heart ached to go to Syd, wrap her in his arms and declare he never wanted to leave. Fear, though, pulsed in his veins like fast moving thorns. She probably hated him. He almost got her killed.

His hands squeezed into fist as he tapped his head on the steering wheel instead. He couldn't think about what would have happened to her if he hadn't arrived at the cabin in time.

How could he face her after that?

Movement at the door alerted him, and he was glad he had turned off the headlights, even if it made him feel like a stalker. He was too far away to see her face clearly, though he wished he could.

She opened the door wider with a sweet note of her voice traveling through his open window, and Guardian pranced inside. Jameson chuckled lightly. She's letting the hairy beast sleep inside.

His smile faded. She's probably letting him inside so she feels safer. Jameson ground his teeth. His doing. He didn't deserve to even think he had a chance with Syd.

He slowly turned the truck around and traveled back out to the highway. Shame coursed through him at his lack of courage. He would have to confront her one day, and soon. Flipping his lights on, the star on his shirt glinted in the reflection.

When Graham had asked him to take the interim position as way to weed out any lingering connections within the department, he thought it was the perfect opportunity to get back to Syd.

Why he ever thought he had the right to intrude upon her life again escaped him. Yet, his heart still tugged to go back to that small house and take Syd in his arms.

He had to figure out a way to make this work.

~*~

The sky still held onto darkness, the sun still far below the mountains, when Sydney loaded up the truck with all of her supplies for the Farm Day event. Homer would be over to milk this morning and take care of the ranch. Once again she thought of having to find help in a couple months. It would be difficult, if not impossible, to find someone to replace him.

"Sorry, boy, I can't bring you on this adventure." She scratched behind Guardian's ears, wishing she could bring the shaggy dog.

He whined as she climbed into the truck. Sydney gave him a wave and signaled for him to stay before driving down the long drive. She flicked her high beams on, but her heart still raced as she rounded the bend in the drive. Every time she drove, she half expected to see a dark SUV at the end of her driveway. Each time there wasn't, she let go of a held breath and chastised herself for holding onto unneeded drama.

The drive to the county fairgrounds where Farm Day was held only took twenty-five minutes at this time of morning. She liked to get there early, get set up, and have her safe spot before the crowds began to arrive.

The sky lightened as she drove down the deserted highway. Mountains rose in the distance, snow now only dressing their top-most peaks. Peace filled her. She may have lost the man that could have completed her life, but she had a ranch nestled in a beautiful valley, animals to care for, pets who loved her, and so much to be grateful for. Today she chose to be grateful and focus on the new business relationships she could make. Maybe she might even meet some young, reliable man looking for work.

A few other vendors waved a hello to her as she pulled up and began unloading her truck. While she struggled with a large load, an older teenage boy rushed over.

"Let me help you, Miss Sydney."

"Why thank you, Jay." Sydney let him take the folding table from her hands. "Sometimes I think I'm stronger than I am."

"Oh, you could have handled it, but I am happy to help."

"You're a sweet young man," she said. The kid blushed. "What are you, a senior now?"

"Just about to graduate." He grinned from ear to ear.

"Well, congratulations. You heading off to college?"

"No, ma'am. I plan to take over my father's ranch, but he wants me to gain some work experience off the ranch first."

Sydney stopped in her tracks. Could her prayer really be answered?

"You okay, Miss Sydney?"

"Yes," she said as she started walking again.

Jay helped her set up the table and the few other things she had brought on that trip from the truck.

"You have more?" Jay asked.

"Plenty more."

"Well, let's go get it. I already set up my parents' booth so I got nothing to do until we open."

They walked together to her truck. Sydney kept glancing at the kid. His family had a cattle ranch, the one that traded with her. Jay had always been a polite guy, saying hello, helping her carry the meat in, and taking the goat from her, not giving her a hard time for her tearful goodbyes.

The kid was tall, lean, and had hands that might one day grow to be as big as Jameson's. Her heart ached for a moment, but she chose to keep her mind focused on gratitude.

"What's next?" Jay asked, watching her with a curious smile.

"What kind of work experience are you looking for, Jay?" She held her breath.

"Any kind of ranch work." He shoved his hands into his pockets. "You looking for another hand?"

"Yes, I am, actually."

Jay's grin widened. "Would you, uh, could I interview for it?"

Sydney laughed. "Jay, you just tell me when you can start, and I'll give you a paid, working interview."

"Really? Well, all be, this is great news! Thank you."

"You don't know how much pressure you took off of me. I am looking forward to it."

"Well, let's get you unloaded. I can't wait to tell my Dad I already have a job, and he thought it would be hard." Jay shook his head as he pulled out a box full of soaps. "Will you teach me how to make the soaps and cheeses?"

"Jay, I'll teach you whatever you want to know about a goat ranch."

Sydney unloaded another box of soaps. She carried it with a lightness in her steps. Gratefulness filled her and she sent up a silent thank you. By the fifth trip to the truck, she wished that she would sell all of her inventory so she didn't have to make so many trips back to the truck. She might not have Jay's help then. She laughed at herself, wishing away for trivial things now.

Jay didn't leave her side until they completely set up her booth. It would be nice to have such an eager young man helping her out on the ranch. He had such a positive, easy-going demeanor, too.

When people started showing up to the fair, Sydney didn't have to force her smile. It came freely. People flocked to her booth. By lunch time, she only had a handful of cheeses left and a box of soaps. Her second wish had practically come true too. With a daring, let-it-all-out-there thought, she laughed. Why not wish for what her heart really wanted?

While squatting to grab some cheese to refill her sample plate, she closed her eyes. *If there is any possible way for Jameson and me to be together, please bring him back into my life.* She smiled at her ridiculousness as she rose with the cheese.

"Hello," an unfamiliar and deep voice greeted her.

She looked up and found dark brown eyes meeting hers. "Hello," she said as she placed the cheese on the sample plate. "Would you like to try a sample of goat cheese?"

"If it's what's making you smile like that, I better."

A blush filled her cheeks. If only he knew where her

smile had come from. She handed a sample to the man, noticing that he didn't have a ring on his finger. She scanned his face again. There weren't many unattached local men in her county.

"You're not from here, are you?" she asked in polite conversation.

"You are perceptive," he said before eating the sample. "Mmmm. This is the best goat cheese I have ever tasted. Did you make this yourself?"

"Yes, it's an old family recipe." She smiled in pride. Aunt Mag and Uncle Joe would be proud of how well their cheese still sold.

"What's your production like?"

"My production?" She cocked her head.

"Yes, how many goats do you have? How many workers? How much cheese can you produce on a monthly basis?"

"Wow, those are quite personal questions, Mr....?" Sydney took a step back. She had never been asked so many demanding questions about her cheese making capabilities.

"Personal, my dear, would be asking why you aren't wearing a wedding ring." He winked at her. "Dean Hadley." He held out his hand.

"Sydney Campbell." She returned his handshake to which he gave an appreciative eyebrow raise.

"I own a chain of grocery stores in Cody. I would love to have some of your fresh goat cheese selling in my stores."

"Oh," she said, dawning realization pinking her cheeks. "I understand now."

Dean smiled and nodded. "Do you have a large enough production to supply me with 1000 ounces a month?"

"I'm hiring some extra help in the next month or so. If you give me time to prepare, I think I can handle that Mr. Hadley."

"Please, call me, Dean. Now, may I ask a personal

question?"

Sydney's breath caught. He was handsome and seemed genuinely nice, but her heart belonged to Jameson, even if he wasn't there to claim it.

"Why hasn't someone grabbed you up yet?"

She lowered her eyes and busied herself by restacking the soaps. "I appreciate the thought, Mr. Had—Dean, but I, my heart belongs to another. It just wouldn't be fair."

"You are an open, honest woman. I admire that." He leaned over and slipped a card on the table. "If you ever give up on him, just let me know. Call me when you have our first order ready. I look forward to doing business with you, Sydney."

When she met his eyes, he smiled genuinely, winked, and strolled on to the next booth.

Sydney's heart lurched. She wished Jameson was here with her, because the truth was, she probably would never give up on him. The table gave her the perfect shield while she squatted, trying to look busy while blinking back the tears. She had too much to be grateful for today to spend this time in a pity party.

Closing her eyes, she did her best to focus on all the wonderful things that had happened, but Jameson kept slipping into her thoughts. So strongly, in fact, that she swore she could smell him and feel his presence.

"How long would it have taken before you gave up?" The rich, deep voice sent chills of delight down her spine.

She squeezed her eyes shut even more. It had to be a dream, but the spark that shot through her as he touched her shoulder told her it was real. She took a sharp breath in.

"Jameson." Whispering his name gave her strength, but she still squeezed her eyes shut.

He squatted next to her, brushed a finger down her temple to her chin. "Open those beautiful eyes, Syd. I'm here."

She slowly opened her eyes and took in the brilliant

green ones staring with adoration down upon her. "You're okay?" Relief poured through.

"More than okay." His gaze captured hers.

"You came back."

"I always keep my promises." He held a hand out to her and helped her up. "Are you going to answer my question?"

She cocked her head.

"How long before you would have given up on me?" His eyes held seriousness, even though the corner of his mouth quirked in that sideways grin that always touched her.

"Never," she said simply.

Jameson put a hand on either side of her face and rested his forehead on hers. "I'm very happy to hear that."

He kissed the tip of her nose and then with one last long look deep into her eyes, he took her lips in his. He kissed her as a man who knew exactly what he wanted, a man who would do whatever was necessary to get it, and a man who knew how to treat a woman.

Sydney's knees shook with emotion. Her wish had come true, again. Her unexpected cowboy had returned to her, and right here in the middle of Farm Day. He claimed her, and she didn't mind one bit.

After a moment, a sharp pressure on her chest made her step back. She looked down at the cause. A sheriff's star shone on Jameson's beige shirt. She stared at it a moment more, looked up at his green eyes shining with mischievousness, and then back at the star.

Jameson was the new sheriff?

~*~

Jameson saw the confusion and then the dawning on Sydney's face. He had hoped to surprise her at home where they had privacy, but when he saw her at the booth, his heart raced and palms sweated. He couldn't wait. He had to see her, and smell her, and hold her in his arms.

He had strode over towards the booth just in time to

hear the end of her conversation with the sharply dressed businessman. His fists clenched against his sides and his heart felt like it would rip from his chest. The moment Syd had told the man that her heart belonged to another, a soothing balm eased his hands and his heart. A warming began then, filling his entire body until he felt on fire—on fire for Sydney Campbell.

With her back in his arms, he felt as if he could take on the world, and he intended to keep it that way. He saw the moment of panic in her eyes as she looked back at the star.

"A compromise?" He touched the star, flipping it up towards him. It felt odd wearing his badge for all to see. "It's only interim, until the next election."

"You gave up the FBI?" She took a step back and blinked rapidly.

He hoped the tears she fought back were happy ones.

"Yes, many of my memories may have returned, but I am different now. I no longer desire that high adrenaline, danger-filled career. I liked the idea of this interim position as a transition."

"What do you want then?" she asked, and he noticed she held her breath.

"A simple, small-town life, with a beautiful, strong woman to walk it with."

"Aww," a crowd whispered and then clapped their hands.

Sydney stepped back, stumbling into Jameson's arms. He pulled her tight into him, his mind reeling. Why hadn't he noticed the crowd gathering? Sydney turned her eyes towards him. That's why. When she looked at him, nothing else in the world mattered.

"Uh, Miss Sydney?" A lanky, but promising looking kid, took a step towards them and cleared his throat. "Would you like me to take over your booth so that you and Sheriff Walsh can catch up without the town watching?"

"You are such a gift, Jay." Sydney squeezed the kid's

hand, and then took Jameson's and led him out into the parking lot to the sounds of cheers.

"Guess I have to get used to this small-town living." Jameson chuckled.

"Walsh, huh?" She knocked into him playfully.

"I have so much to share with you, Syd. I have wonderful parents, and a brother and sister, and an energetic nephew. I spent summers on my Uncle's farm, like you did."

"No wife, I'm guessing?" she teased.

"No wife, no girlfriend. I guess I was difficult to impress, or so I'm told." He shrugged. According to his fellow agents, he was all work and no play. They had tired of his lack of interest in the dates they tried to set him up with and stopped even asking. "I just hadn't met the right woman yet."

Sydney laughed, pure joy bubbling forth. He loved her laugh. It sent his heart in rapid fire, and he wanted to bottle it up to keep it with him always.

It had taken too long to get back to her. The debriefing took ten times as long because of his amnesia. Though many of his memories had returned, he still couldn't remember the months leading up to waking up on the side of the road. It frustrated his superiors, but they still had O'Neal.

Graham was dismayed to receive his letter of resignation, but he nodded his understanding. *A good woman can change you*, he had said. Jameson knew it would take more than just a two-week notice. When dealing with national security, there was a lot more paperwork and interviews.

The process only confirmed that he had made the right choice. He wanted a simpler life, one filled with physical work, no stress about losing his life or that of others, or having to take them. He wanted to be surrounded by the woman he loved…and maybe even a little one or two. He smiled with the thought of little Sydneys running around—

little girls in dirty dresses riding their ponies bareback.

"What's that look all about?" Sydney asked as they reached her truck.

"Just imagining a future…" he trailed off, lost in his imaginations again.

"A future?"

He blinked, settling his focus on her eyes. "A future with you, starting with that dinner I promised."

# ~Epilogue~

The chill of the morning burned off as the sun shone down on the ranch, her ranch. Sydney breathed in the fresh scent of newly green grass and wild flowers. Of course the goats and horses added their own essence to the mix, but it brought her comfort.

She strolled along her property behind her house where they had planted a lawn nestled within her garden area. The view of the mountains shooting up in the distance was unhindered here, and beautiful. Their snow-capped peaks gleamed in the sun.

Jameson had also set up a fire pit area here. Her hand touched the sanded wood of the bench he had made for her. It leaned far back so they could stargaze to their hearts' content. A wash of warmth flooded her with the memory of being held in his arms, watching the shooting stars with the fire crackling near their feet.

It couldn't get more romantic, especially since this spot gave him the perfect setting to propose.

Sydney had teased him, that he had built that spot for just the purpose of his grand proposal. It worked though. Her thumb caressed the simple engagement ring that he had given her. The diamond was set back into the ring so it wouldn't catch on anything while she worked. His thoughtfulness touched her almost as much as the words he had said.

"I would wake up without my memory a thousand more times if I needed to, for it's what brought me to you, the love of my life, my home, and my future." His words had ingrained themselves into her soul.

For a man of few words, Jameson knew how to use the

ones he spoke effectively.

She scanned the lush area again, grateful for Jameson's idea to create such a reprieve. Her eyes landed on the archway, and her heart raced. Today, under that canopy of jasmine, she would promise her life to Jameson's, and he would promises his to her, and he always kept his promises. She didn't have any fear or misgivings about the day, only excitement and yearning to build a future with the man who held her heart.

Jameson had already expressed his desire to have children. The thought caused heat to fill Sydney's cheeks. Having a couple little ones running around the ranch did sound like it completed their perfect picture. It would have made Aunt Mag and Uncle Joe happy. She could almost feel them smiling down at her from heaven.

Sydney walked through the garden, touching the buds forming on the flowers that would soon turn into tomatoes and squash, and so much more. A sweet smell called to her and she meandered her way over to the small flower garden Jameson planted for her on her birthday just a month ago.

She didn't have to blow candles out on her own that night, and she made sure to be very careful about her wish.

The peace of the moment steadied her heart, and she closed her eyes to memorize it. In only a matter of moments, her quiet life would be descended upon by family and friends. Her parents had actually made their way out for the wedding, and Jameson put them up in a hotel twenty minutes down the road.

"The house will be ours tonight. We have no need to share it." His wink made Sydney blush, and she had playfully pushed past him to finish her chores.

Gravel popping on the road, and Guardian's deep woof, alerted her to her peaceful moment's end. A couple doors slammed, but she didn't want to move.

"Sydney!" Jameson's mom called out. "Where is my favorite soon-to-be daughter-in-law?"

Sydney felt the smile tug on her lips. She had fallen in love with Jameson's family the moment she met them, and it seemed that they returned that love. His mom, a strong, assertive woman, doted on her and instantly took her under her wing. His laid-back dad always had a funny joke and jolly laugh to share. His sister treated her as the sister she always wished she had, and his brother teased her just like she thought a brother would. And that nephew of his, well, she could just gobble that sweet boy up.

With one last deep breath of her garden and the peace it lent her, she strolled around her house. Jameson's sister saw her first and immediately clasped arms with her.

"We brought the perfect accessories to go with your dress."

"And Jameson insisted that he pick the wildflowers for your bouquet." His mom held up a beautiful and brilliant bouquet of Indian paint brush, lupine, and other native flowers. "Let's put them in some water so they stay fresh for the ceremony."

"This is so exciting! I can't believe Jameson is finally getting married!" His sister pulled her into the house. "We only have two hours until the guests begin to arrive, so we better get started!"

By the time the guests began to amble in, Sydney stood in her simple, tulle, white dress. She touched the skirt, trying to remember the last time she wore one. It felt odd, yet at the same time reminded her of how feminine she could feel, if she wanted.

Jameson's sister practically hopped around in excitement, and though his mom remained stoic, thrill lit her eyes. Sydney had watched the guests arrive, and even got a glimpse of her handsome groom, before his sister pulled her, insisting she not create bad luck.

Sydney excused herself to the bathroom. Her heart fluttered and her hands shook. Looking at her reflection, she barely recognized herself. She touched the silky curls that had been put in her hair. She blinked her makeup-darkened eyes, smacked her lipsticked mouth, and fingered the fancy necklace her soon-to-be mother-in-law had brought her. Would Jameson like what he saw? Would he recognize her? Would he expect her to dress like this more often? She laughed. No, he knew her, and he loved her for the hard-working, jean-wearing, no-makeup girl that she was.

She blew out a deep breath. Today she was getting married.

In a matter of minutes now she would be Mrs. Jameson Walsh. The name had a ring to it, she nodded, like it was meant to be. She sent a silent thank you to her Aunt Mag and Uncle Joe. As much as she wished they could be with her right now, she knew they watched from heaven with smiles.

A soft knock stirred Sydney from her thoughts.

She opened the door to see her mother. It was the first time she had seen her in over two years. She hadn't changed much, maybe a few more strands of gray in her long, dark hair, a few more lines around her eyes and mouth, but otherwise no difference…except when her hazel eyes met Sydney's, they brimmed with tears.

"Look at you!" her mother exclaimed. "You are radiant!"

"Thanks, mom," Sydney said, feeling almost shy. Her mother had never been one for open compliments. "I'm glad you and dad could make it."

"How could we miss our only child's wedding?"

For a split second Sydney wanted to combat with, how could you miss your only child's birthday two years in a row? But the tears welling in her mother's eyes stopped the words in her mouth. No need to go into that today. She was getting married. Although she hadn't thought about how magical a wedding should be since she was a very young girl, she found she wished it could be so today. She wished for one day, she could feel like that princess she never would be.

Her dad walked down the hall towards them. She could hear his heavy, lazy steps. "Where's my little girl?"

Sydney felt her own eyes well then. He hadn't called her his little girl for a very long time.

"She's no longer a girl, Stan, just look at her." Her mother dabbed at her eyes.

"Well, look at this. My little girl has blossomed into a fairy-tale princess." He took Sydney into a hug, and she let him, soaking in the feeling she had wished for so long.

There is just something about daddies and their little girls. She always sought his approval and today she felt like she had it.

"You have done a nice job of fixing this place up, Syd." He nodded. "Joe would be mighty proud of you."

"Thanks, Dad. I hope so."

"It's time!" Jameson's mom called from the living room.

"I guess it's time," Sydney repeated, pulling on her dress and doing her best to keep her heart from racing right out of her.

"You'll let me give you away?" her dad asked, the slightest quiver in his voice. "I know I haven't been perfect, but I always did my best," he leaned in and whispered.

"I know, Dad," Sydney said, blinking rapidly and laying a hand on his arm.

"This is so beautiful," her mom sing-songed. "Oh, I better get in my place." She patted Sydney's arm and then half-ran out of the house.

"Us too," Jameson's mom smiled at her. "You look amazing, Syd. We are so lucky to be welcoming you into our family today." She kissed Sydney on the cheek and then strode out the door shouting for other participants to get into place even before the screen slammed shut.

His sister said, "I'm walking right in front of you two. Jameson's handsome FBI friend is walking me." Jenny hardly kept in the squeal.

"Rick is a nice guy, Jenny," Sydney said, smiling to herself. She had gotten to know Rick and a few other of Jameson's friends over the last year.

"Meow," Mr. Paws spoke up and rubbed under her dress.

Sydney bent down to give him a few pets. Then she stood, took a deep breath, slipped her hand in her dad's offered arm, and walked into her new life.

Guardian walked with her down the aisle. She could hear a few chuckles and comments about her sidekick, but she loved that he stood by her. When Jameson met her gaze, his eyes went wide in appreciation. Once their eyes locked, everything else faded into a muted background. She hardly even heard the vows and promises they made to each other. She knew them by heart though, and their meanings would always exist inside of her.

~*~

An angel. He was marrying an angel. That was the only thought going through Jameson's head ever since he saw Syd walking towards him in that flowing white dress. A beautiful, multi-colored eyed, hard-working, strong angel. The woman who saved him in too many ways to count.

The crowd of people that had been causing him to pull at his tux's collar for the last twenty minutes faded off into the distance. They ceased to exist.

When Syd's dad handed her to him, Jameson bent close to her ear and whispered, "I am the luckiest man on this earth."

He was awarded with a beautiful pink flush that faded out her freckles as she shyly looked down at their hands intertwined. Her strong hands gripped his as if she needed his strength to help her pull through. The feeling warmed Jameson. He loved knowing that this strong, independent woman still needed him.

His thumb caressed the back of her hand as the pastor began the ceremony. He had memorized his vows and all he would say, but the act became like a fuzzy dream.

In a matter of moments, Sydney would be his for the rest of their lives. His heart raced with the thought, the same sensation that had begun the moment she met him at the door with a shotgun aimed at his heart. A smile tugged its way across his lips. He didn't know what it was that led him towards that moment in time, whether it was a wish as Syd confessed to him awhile back, fate, God, or whatever, he knew he had been meant to be with the angel in his arms.

~*~

Not even a year later…

Syd thrummed her fingers on the kitchen table. Her heart raced and she looked again towards the bathroom where the stick still sat on the counter. When the popping of gravel sounded in the driveway she stood in a rush. The world turned black for a moment, so she steadied herself with one hand holding the table for support, the table that brought so many good memories to her.

Jameson was home.

Her mind spun with all the ways she could tell him. He had wanted this from the very beginning. He asked for it on their wedding night, but would reality sing a different tune? Her head swam with so many unknowns.

Jameson strode from his Sheriff's truck like a man with an agenda. Uh-oh, her news may have to wait…

~*~

Jameson couldn't wait to get home to Syd. He was so excited to tell her that his body was full of adrenaline. He thought she would be happy, almost positive. That thought gave him a little pause as he slowed to greet Guardian.

"Hey boy, did you protect Syd today? Good boy." He smiled, loving how he started talking to the animals like Syd did. "Wife, I'm home!" he said with a laugh as he came through the door.

"I don't think I'll ever tire of you calling me that,

Husband." Sydney fell into his arms and kissed him, just a little longer than normal. "How was your day?"

"You ask like we didn't talk several times." He chuckled and kissed her once more. "Why are you so fidgety?"

Sydney wrapped her fingers around each other and shrugged. "Why were you in such a rush to get inside?"

"What, can't a man be excited to see his wife after the end of a long day?"

Syd eyed him. She knew him too well.

"Okay. Okay. So, it's time to elect a new Sheriff, and you know I've been going back and forth about what to do. Should I run or not?"

Syd nodded, and her eyes widened. She squeezed her lips together like she held back a secret, but he had to keep going.

"I know it's been difficult with all the crazy calls in the middle of the night for cows going missing and such. I feel like I missed out on a big part of the kidding time." He paused to take a breath. "Well, I've decided that I want to ranch full-time with you."

Syd blew out a long breath, a look of relief washing over her face. Phew. Jameson allowed his body to relax as he realized he made the right decision. He hoped that was what she had wanted, and he hoped that working with her might relieve enough stress she could finally get pregnant.

"You're okay with that?" he asked her.

"You're timing couldn't be more perfect." She smiled in an I-have-a-fantastic-surprise-for-you kind of way.

"You going to tell me why?"

Syd opened her mouth, closed it, and giggled.

"Come on, Syd. I'm dying here." He felt like it. For some reason his adrenaline began to pound even faster than before. His face felt hot and his hands began to sweat.

"I'm pregnant!"

Jameson blinked, trying to decipher if he heard her

correctly. They had been trying for almost a year now, and he was beginning to wonder if there was a problem. But no…they were having a baby! He picked her up and twirled her around.

"Really? You're sure?" He gazed deep into her beautiful, mysterious eyes.

She nodded, ran back to the bathroom, and came back with a white stick. "Two pink lines."

Sure enough, two bright pink lines lit the indentation in the pregnancy test.

Once again everything seemed to line up for them. He brought his wife to him, held her tightly, and then laid a hand on her belly. They were starting a family.

~*~

Sydney tip-toed quietly out of the room. She had laid their six-month-old son down in his crib next to his big sister's bed. She slept like an angel, sun-washed hair spread like a halo on her pillow. With a sigh, Sydney watched her beautiful children. She had been blessed. Both of her kids were sound sleepers. Of course, it could be the long hours playing and working on the ranch that made them sleep so well.

She smiled at the thought. Her Aunt Mag always said there was no better cure for insomnia than a good ol' day on the ranch.

With one last, longing look at her two blessings, she slipped down the hall to her bedroom. Jameson sat in the glow of the computer screen, typing away on the keyboard. She wrapped her arms around him and kissed him on the neck.

"Anything interesting on Unforgettable Cowboys tonight?" She had encouraged him to reach out to other people with amnesia, to help him deal with the fact that he still couldn't remember some things, especially the months before he woke up on the side of the road. The support forum he found online was called Unforgettable Cowboys: A Wyoming Amnesia Support Group.

"Actually, yes." He titled his head back to kiss her on the lips. "The kids go down easy?"

"Always. We're blessed."

"Yes, we are." He kissed her again and then refocused on the computer.

"So, what's so interesting?" She sat at the edge of the bed, still close enough to touch him.

"There's a new member. He has taken it upon himself to take in a gal who had an accident right in front of him. She has no memory of who she is, where she's from, nothing. He rescued her before her car tumbled over into a deep canyon. It's irretrievable, at least until after winter."

"Wow, it's amazing he was able to save her."

"I agree." He nodded.

"So, she's okay, other than amnesia?"

"She has some injuries, but nothing more serious than some broken bones."

"That is pretty interesting. Not too far from our own story." She leaned up and kissed his head.

"It gets even more remarkable."

"Yeah?"

"She thinks she remembers him."

"But no one else?" Sydney cocked her head.

"Well, the thing is, they had never even really met. She dropped her purse at a restaurant, and he helped her pick it up before she drove off, all only minutes before the accident."

"So what advice are you giving him?"

"I don't know much, just to give her time and try to jar her memory with questions and helping her find her family." His eyebrows furrowed.

"That's pretty heavy stuff."

"Not as heavy as what I brought along with me." He typed a farewell and then shutdown the computer.

"Well, we handled it. Or I should say, you handled it."

Jameson pulled her up into an embrace. "We handled it together. I don't know where I would be without you."

"And I you," she said, wrapping her arms around him.

In his arms she always felt safe, like she was right where she belonged and nothing else mattered. Whether it was her wish that started this all or not, she would be forever grateful that her unexpected cowboy ended up on her doorstep all those years ago. Her life had only increasingly become more and more rewarding and full of love.

*******

Thank you for reading Her Unexpected Cowboy. I hope you enjoyed Jameson's and Sydney's story!

I love hearing from my readers, so please leave me a review! I read each and every one!

Here are the links for reviews:

Amazon:
https://www.amazon.com/B07NZZ1NSR/
BookBub:
https://www.bookbub.com/books/her-unexpected-cowboy-unforgettable-cowboys-book-1-by-danae-c-little
Goodreads:
https://www.goodreads.com/book/show/44103077-her-unexpected-cowboy?from_search=true

# NEXT in Unforgettable Cowboys
# Sweet Romance Series

A Clean & Wholesome Cowboy Romance

**Kay's only memory is from a dream of a cowboy she has never actually met.**

Kay is running, but from what she doesn't know. In the midst of her escape she loses her memory and everything from her past. The only thing she has left is a necklace with a pendant of her name and a reoccurring dream of a cowboy. The cowboy who rescued her.

Curt McAlister is intrigued by the woman with flighty green eyes. She captivates him enough that when he runs to her rescue, he takes on the title of her fiancé to ensure she makes it through.

Will Curt be able to explain the truth before Kay's past catches up with them? Or will his heart keep the lie he desperately wants to be the truth?

Coming May 2019!

# Reach Out!

**I love to hear from my readers! Reach out on Facebook or leave a review. Let me know your favorite book of mine!**

**Join Danae's Reader Group for new release announcements and receive a FREE book!
https://mybookcave.com/d/c04ceb22/**

**Waiting for Her Dream Cowboy? Have you read my More Than Friends series yet?**

**Start with Book One:**

More Than My Billionaire Boss
He needs a girlfriend.  She is his devout assistant. One kiss changes it all.
Read Now:
https://www.amazon.com/dp/B07JFLC2TS

# More Books by Danae Little:

Fiction:

More Than Friends Sweet Romance series:

More Than My Billionaire Boss:
https://www.amazon.com/dp/B07JFLC2TS
More Than My Ex-Fiancé:
https://www.amazon.com/dp/B07JB473LK/
More Than My Brother's Best Friend:
https://www.amazon.com/dp/B07JHG4JPW/
More Than My Country Star Crush:
https://www.amazon.com/dp/B07KNLS2G3/
More Than My Playboy Co-Worker:
https://www.amazon.com/dp/B07L7W2LCS/

Unforgettable Cowboys:

Her Unexpected Cowboy
https://www.amazon.com/dp/B07NZZ1NSR/
Her Dream Cowboy
Coming May 2019!

Homestead series:

Finding Home (Homestead Book One):
https://www.amazon.com/dp/B0773RY9R5/
A Walk in Matt's Shoes (Homestead Book Two):
https://www.amazon.com/dp/B07D1CT9RW

Misplaced Love:
https://www.amazon.com/dp/B07174G5M2/

Children's:

Doesn't Everyone Love Dragons?:
https://www.amazon.com/dp/B01M750HPZ/

Keepsake Journals:

Did You Hear That?:
https://www.amazon.com/dp/1533431566/
Did You See That?:
https://www.amazon.com/dp/1533452393
Baby Blessings:
https://www.amazon.com/dp/1537644769/

Guided Journals:

Write Your Marriage Back Together:
https://www.amazon.com/dp/1544187289
Daily Marriage Appreciations Journal:
https://www.amazon.com/dp/1544923333/
Marriage Problem Solving Journal:
https://www.amazon.com/dp/1544707347/

Memoir:

Carson's Gifts:
https://www.amazon.com/dp/B00DFMGE5K/

Non-Fiction:

Interactive Classroom Management: Interactive Tools:
https://www.amazon.com/dp/B01G7SW42U/

# ABOUT THE AUTHOR

Danae Little writes sweet, clean romance as well as some women's fiction. Each book that she writes holds an element of hope that leaves her readers saying, "Aww!" at the end of the story.

Danae Little lives in a small town at the base of the Sierra's with the adventurous love of her life and their miraculous son. She spends her days feeling blessed to be chasing imaginary dragons in their magical forest and finding any quiet moment possible to put pen to paper.

Follow Danae on:

Facebook
http://www.facebook.com/danaelittleauthor

Twitter
http://www.twitter.com/dclittleauthor

BookBub
https://www.bookbub.com/authors/danae-c-little

Newsletter
http://eepurl.com/dIyRR9

Join Danae's VIP Readers
https://www.facebook.com/groups/1043326012501406/

DISCARD

Made in the USA
Monee, IL
24 March 2023

30472656R00104